The Lost Summer

A Wishing Star Book

The Lost Summer

Joan Oppenheimer

SCHOLASTIC BOOK SERVICES

New York Toronto London Auckland Sydney Tokyo

To the Tuesday Workshop Group,
with gratitude and love

Cover Photo by Owen Brown

ISBN 0-590-32132-3

12 11 10 9 8 7 6 5   1 2/8

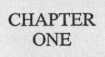

CHAPTER ONE

Susie Kettering sat in the back of the room for her last period class, Sophomore English. On this particular afternoon, a soft around-the-corner-from-summer day in May, she found it a distinct hardship to stay awake, much less pay attention to the teacher.

Miss Blake was a wispy little woman without a sense of humor or any style whatsoever in teaching a subject Susie had always found dull. The teacher's low droning voice made her sleepy even on days that weren't as nice as this one. More often than not, in all her classes, Susie sat bored and vaguely unhappy about the way her life was going.

Today, she had really tried to follow the review lecture, well aware that she was just squeaking by in English. But at last she succumbed to the balmy air coming through the window that brushed her cheek with a warm feathery touch. She thought drowsily, who needed school? Especially at the end of May after the usual rotten winter.

Then she remembered that it was Friday, and her spirits lifted. There would be a park party, without Mark this time to glare at her if she had a couple of drinks, arguing about it, spoiling everything. She'd have a lot more fun without him, that was for sure.

Susie's pencil doodled its way down the page from her first conscientious notes. Drifting into daydreams, she began a sketch of her best friend, two rows away and three seats ahead.

La Dawn wore a pantsuit that was almost the same shade as her skin. Chocolate colored, Susie thought. *Melted* chocolate with a sheen to it. La Dawn might join in the chorus of complaints about skin problems from the girls in their crowd, but it was obvious she had nothing to worry about.

Susie signed her name beneath the sketch, a large, swirling, barely legible "Susie." She sat frowning at it, lost in a line of thought she had pursued many times before. Funny thing about names, they either seemed to fit beautifully or not at all. Did people make a conscious effort to be like their names, she wondered, or maybe as unlike them as possible?

Her own name certainly didn't fit her, not in any way. Anybody named Susie should be little and chirpy and cute, not tall and slender and still waiting for something to develop, hopefully a figure. Neither was she a Susan, someone poised and elegant and sophisticated.

Actually, Susie thought of herself as still getting her act together, just over the line from the tomboy stage. It had been so neat up to sixth grade, being best friends with La Dawn and Pam Lyon, living on the same block, playing together, sleeping at each other's houses.

Uncomplicated fun, nothing really bad or sad, none of the feeling of things changing too fast. That came later, along with all the emotional churning inside, the doubts about measuring up. If only she had realized then how wonderful, how perfect life had been.

It was good, of course, that she had not been able to look into the future to her father's death three years ago when she was thirteen. Or to a time — six months ago now — when her mother ruined everything, just as they were doing so well, by marrying Casey Sears.

Hastily, Susie shoved Casey into a dark corner of her mind, wishing there were some way to keep him there, to stop thinking about him so much. It only made it worse, chewing at herself with anger and resentment.

There was another reason it was just as well she had not been able to project into the future to now when she felt barely adequate. She wore her curly brown hair long. It was hair with a mind of its own, stubborn about not looking right sometimes. Her skin had been pretty much okay of late, though she hated being so fair that she sunburned easily in the summer.

La Dawn liked to tease her about that. "We all know black is beautiful," she would say, "but you're never gonna make it, babe. Not all in one day, for sure."

La Dawn was somebody whose name was *insanely* wrong, though Susie secretly respected her for not shortening it to Dawn. Most kids would have done that. Maybe she would have, too. But La Dawn seemed to have that kind of thing in perspective, saving her energy for more important matters.

She was a really pretty girl, fine-boned, smaller than Susie and with no more figure, but it didn't seem to matter as much. La Dawn was more in proportion, so it never looked as if there were a definite deficiency, as Susie was convinced it did in her case.

She sat for a moment, checking her sketch against the live model. Enormous brown eyes, sweeping curly lashes, a button nose, and wide full lips. When La Dawn smiled, the whole world smiled back, because almost everyone liked her.

Actually, when Susie stopped to think about the three-way friendship they had with each other and Pam, she figured one reason it had endured might be because they were all so different. She and La Dawn felt kind of big-sisterish toward cute, plump, little Pam, who never seemed to concentrate for twenty con-

4

secutive seconds on anything but boys.

La Dawn and Susie worried somewhat about it, even talked by the hour to Pam. Everything sailed over her honey-blonde head, however, and for a very simple reason. She didn't consider being boy-crazy any problem at all.

The bell rang, jolting Susie out of her reflections. She watched La Dawn, waiting patiently until the stampede had gone by and the room was clear.

Then she turned and grinned. "Anybody'd think it was Friday," she said in her soft lazy voice. "Here's the assignment." She handed Susie a slip of paper.

"Thanks. I didn't even hear it."

La Dawn looked up at her and shook her head, but she was still smiling. "You better hit your books this weekend," she said.

They were halfway to their lockers before she asked the question Susie had been expecting all day. "Did you make up with Mark?"

Susie made a face. "Billy Graham, Jr.? Forget it. I am so sick of him hassling me at every single party. I get enough of that at home. 'Why can't you be like so-and-so? Why don't you work harder — up to your potential?' "

She gestured sharply. "I'm tired of that line, too. You'd think Nora would have the message by now. She doesn't know the first thing about me, let alone my fabulous potential."

La Dawn glanced at her, but said nothing.

Susie brightened. "Are you and Tony coming to the park tonight?"

5

"I suppose so. Want us to stop by for you?"

"No, I'll walk over. Did Scott Carney ever get around to asking Pam?"

La Dawn nodded. "She's been walking into walls all day. If you talk to her, remember it's 'Stage One.' Don't expect her to make much sense."

Susie laughed. "They look so funny together. Somebody the size of the Jolly Green Giant and little old Pam, about up to his shirt pocket. Well, if she's happy — "

La Dawn touched her arm. "I wish you were," she said, her eyes sober. "If you could just — not let your dad bother you so much — "

"He is not my dad," Susie said between clenched teeth. "He's my mother's husband. And if he'd ever get over this perfectly weird idea that a stepfather has some kind of special role to play — somebody midway between a friend and a parent, someone I can communicate with — " She stressed the words with acid scorn. "I'd find life a whole lot more beautiful if he would just get — off — my — case."

"Yeah," La Dawn said without expression. "Yeah, well — I've got to get to the library. See you tonight, okay?"

She had started Susie thinking again about the most recent upheaval in her life, the thing she dwelled on too much, too often. It made her churn inside with dark violent frustration, but she couldn't seem to stop going over it again and again.

6

She knew too well by now that it was an exercise in futility, recalling her father's death three years ago. It had been a dreadfully vulnerable time to lose somebody she loved so much.

She had never told him how much he meant to her, either. At thirteen, your parents were just — there. You knew they'd always be there. You'd have the rest of your life to tell them that you loved them. She tasted regret once more, bitter, salty, like unshed tears.

Occasionally, she searched her memory frantically for the way her father had looked, tall and angular with dark hair. But what color had his eyes been? What did he look like when he smiled? She would feel a moment of panic before his face finally came clear in her mind.

Of course. His eyes were hazel like hers, and he had smiled slowly but easily. He smoked a pipe, so he smelled of tobacco and the peppermints he loved, and sometimes of a woodsy, heathery aftershave that Nora liked. She said it suited him. So, after being married to a great person like that, how could she have settled for somebody like Casey?

Susie dove into her locker, scattering papers and books so that they spilled over onto the floor. Around her, shrill voices rose and fell, chattering, squealing, laughing, making plans for the weekend ahead. But the clamor faded into a backdrop for the pictures in her mind, all the more vivid because of the strength of her anger.

She didn't remember much about her father's funeral, mercifully blocked in her memory. But she could see with startling clarity the way her mother had looked afterward. A petite, perky, pretty redhead, Nora had looked white and drawn that night, a little more than three years ago.

When everyone had left and the two of them were alone at last in the big house, Susie had begun to cry softly. Her mother's arms went around her, rocking her back and forth for a moment as if she were small again.

"It'll be the two of us now," she said in a low strangled voice, "just the two of us."

Susie took the words to heart, fiercely, literally. There were no other relatives, no aunts or uncles or cousins. Nora's parents were dead, and neither of them had ever met Susie's paternal grandmother, an invalid who lived in Florida.

Well, the two of them had made it okay. If the men who dated her mother didn't measure up in Susie's opinion, she learned a dozen different ways to get rid of them. It was mostly a matter of acting like a complete monster. But she was not above hinting at various mysterious problems, either Nora's or her own, which required constant and expensive medical attention and/or sessions with a psychiatrist.

She informed one interested man, blithely, "Oh, Dr. Parkins is almost like one of the family!"

As the daughter of a doctor and a nurse, she

had enough knowledge of technical terms to pull it off, as a rule. Things had been fine — until Casey Sears came along.

Susie slammed her locker shut and let herself be carried down the corridor on a wave of hurrying students, spilling down the steps and through the doors. Outside, they scurried in all directions, bright flashes of color against a landscape that was still dull and winter-drab.

Susie plodded down the sidewalk in the same measured tempo as her thoughts, which always led to the same distasteful denouement. Casey.

A salesman of medical supplies, he had come to know Nora (who was back working at the hospital) before Susie had a chance to figure out how to discourage him. He wouldn't have been as easy to shake as the others, anyway, she thought, and winced at the vivid picture of him in her mind.

He had a mop of black curly hair and crinkly bright-blue eyes. They always gave her the uncomfortable feeling that he saw a lot more than she felt like revealing, especially to him. His round, tough face was like a fist, with every line and feature carved in flesh as it might have been in stone.

That was Casey, saying to the world, "This is how I am. Like it or go to hell." But then he would grin and the blue eyes would disappear entirely into gleaming slits, shooting occasional sparks of amusement, and the lines in his face would deepen.

"Prematurely aged," he liked to say. "Parents died before I was born. In and out of trouble, love, jail, and a dozen jobs by the time I was 25. Last year, that is."

All lies. Part of the big act that helped him move in on Nora, so fast that Susie didn't realize what was happening until too late. Her mother was beyond reasoning with by that time. They went off and got married, then came home acting as if Susie were a silly, pouty little kid who'd get over being a brat if they just ignored her.

Nora told her quietly, eyes shining with that inner glow that was back again now, "Susie, this has nothing to do with what I felt for your father. That will always be special, a lovely special memory. But he's gone. And — I just couldn't make it by myself any longer."

"You had me," Susie said accusingly. "You said it would be the two of us. And we were getting along great."

Nora sighed, and the light in her eyes dimmed a little.

Good, Susie thought. Her mother used to look that way years ago, so how could it have been so special? Here she was turning it on again — for Casey.

"You don't understand," Nora said. "You probably won't understand till you're grown."

At the time, Susie had written it off to the man-woman thing, though she certainly couldn't see what Casey had that was so terrific, not compared to her father.

But now she'd changed her mind. Nora must be weak, that's all. She couldn't hack it by herself? Well, she hadn't been by herself. She hadn't been alone. There had been two of them, just like she said.

Susie blinked hard, angrily, against the tears that stung behind her eyes.

Despite what La Dawn said, it was when Casey came on the scene that she began drinking at the park parties. That was when it first got heavy. The storm inside her had built gradually, not being able to talk to anybody. Not Nora. Not even La Dawn, who couldn't or wouldn't see things the way they really were, not this time. And Pam was off on Cloud Ninety, as usual.

Susie turned the corner onto South Elm, looked down the street at her house, and felt her eyes mist with tears once more. If only things could go back to the way they were a couple of years ago. Knowing they couldn't was why she drank, for the nice, blurred, fuzzy feeling that took away the hurt and the worry about what was going to happen to her.

She lifted her head, took a deep breath, and quickened her steps. It was Friday, a nice warm day for a park party tonight. And Mark wouldn't be on her back this time.

Susie whispered to herself in what La Dawn called her 'watermelon accent,' "Ever'thin's gon be jes cool. I mean, *cool* — "

11

CHAPTER
TWO

The houses on South Elm were curiously alike, big old-fashioned two-story houses, usually white, most of them in need of paint. But Susie had often noted that the yards were well kept. The families on the block were proud of the enormous old trees, lush summer lawns, shrubbery, and colorful flower beds.

This was an older section of Parkdale, in turn an older suburb west of Chicago. The people on this street had lived here for most of the years in Susie's memory. In fact, La Dawn's family, the Hollands, and two other black families were the only ones she could remember who were new on the street since the time when she was five or six and first began to notice things like that.

Years later, she realized that people who began to make more money moved on to a more fashionable section north of town, or possibly to one of the North Shore suburbs. If her father had lived, they might have had one of those modern houses of stone or mellow brick, perhaps with pillars in a colonial style, back from the road, with winding drives and high walls in front.

There were no homes like that in this part of Parkdale. But Susie loved the old houses on South Elm. She was dimly aware of the fact that the neighborhood was part of her security, perhaps a large part of it since the shattering changes in the structure of her own family.

She didn't like people changing anything about the houses on the street. When Pam Lyon's parents painted their house a kind of silver gray with darker charcoal shutters, it took her weeks to get used to it so that she didn't feel a mild resentment every time she walked by.

Today, she was barely past when Pam came flying out the door, calling to her, "Susie, you'll never guess — "

Susie played it straight, aware of a warm protective feeling toward Pam, the closest thing she had to the little sister she had always wanted.

"What?" she inquired obligingly.

Pam's gray eyes shone. "He asked me!" she said, breathless with excitement. "He asked me to go to the park tonight!"

"He?" Susie put her head to one side. "Jim?

Mike? Greg Livingston? No, they were last week — "

Pam giggled. "Scott Carney, dummy. You never listen when I talk. Worse than my mom. Now she says she'll nick my allowance a dime for every time I mention his name after the first ten times. Oh, but he's so great! Honestly, Susie, isn't he the greatest thing since — "

Words failed her, and she flung out her arms in a rapturous gesture.

Susie nodded solemnly. Her private opinion of Scott would never be shared with the volatile Pam. He was nice enough, an enormous, amiable, shambling young man, inevitably a football star, but without much going for him above the eyebrows.

Maybe he had been on the bottom of too many pileups in too many games, Susie thought, but without malice. Scott was a whole lot better than Greg Livingston, for example, somebody whose crazy-wild reputation endowed him with a certain fascination, especially for types like Pam.

"I'm really glad he asked you," Susie said warmly, "but I figured he would. See? You worried all week for nothing. All that agony wasted."

"Yeah," Pam said dreamily. "Well — I'm running half an hour late, and I have to wash my hair." The last words drifted back over her shoulder as she hurried toward the house.

Susie grinned to herself as she walked on.

Pam was a good kid, unfailingly cheerful, always looking as if she'd put herself together on the way out the door, at least half an hour late for something. She had an older brother and sister, both married, and Susie recalled puzzling for a long time over something she heard Nora say years ago to a neighbor.

"They're both close to fifty. Pam was obviously an afterthought."

Well, it didn't seem to bother her, Susie mused. Maybe she was lucky, being left to her own devices most of the time, nobody caring too much what she did as long as she got average grades and cleaned up her room once a week.

Her parents were graying, pleasant, rather absent-minded people. In fact, they looked so much alike that Susie used to get the giggles when she had dinner at their house. Hilariously, like mirror images, they sat at opposite ends of the table, taking small bites, using their napkins in unison, chewing and swallowing, then reaching for their water or coffee, as if maneuvered by the same inner mechanisms.

Only one thing about them really bothered Susie. That was the way they acted toward La Dawn, gushy, utterly phony, every word and gesture saying, "See how liberal we are? We accept our daughter's friend even though she's black."

At the Lyon's house, the three girls spent most of their time in Pam's room. The subject of her parents' attitude toward the black families on the street was one they ignored by tacit agreement. Susie had once reflected that it was probably more for Pam's sake than La Dawn's.

Unless somebody put her down, La Dawn never made a big deal of the black-white thing. Maybe that was because she had lived in a black neighborhood on the south side of Chicago until she was six. After that, here in Parkdale, she made so many friends that she seemed to shrug off the few kids who didn't accept her. Sure, there had been a few incidents, but La Dawn could take care of herself, summoning the words to show a bully or a bigot up for just what he was.

Even in second grade, Susie recalled, La Dawn had turned on a boy jeering at her Christmas angels which she had colored with brown faces.

"You dumb honky," she told him calmly, "are you in for a surprise!'

Yet, close as they were, Susie sometimes had a glimpse of uncharted, unsuspected depths in La Dawn. Always realistic, though she joked about realities with a funny, wry sense of humor, she never turned her back on a situation, pretending it didn't exist.

"We're movin' up," she liked to say, brown eyes sparkling. "My people are on the mooooove."

But once when Susie complained about discrimination because the boys got to use the gym more frequently and at better hours, La

Dawn looked at her for a long moment.

"Now, what would you know about something like discrimination?" she said quietly.

And there was Brotherbear, La Dawn's beloved childhood toy, a small battered panda. She still kept him on the shelf above her bed. He had lost one button eye, but there was something much more unusual about him. The small La Dawn had taken a bottle of brown liquid shoe polish and dyed all the white portions of the little fuzzy bear.

Over the years, the other two girls teased her about it, once remarking on the brown color, now a rather mottled orange.

"He's half black, half Indian," Susie insisted. "What he is, he's a breed!"

La Dawn grinned. "What can I tell you? Takes some kind of thinking to come up with a statement like that," she drawled. "Takes a super-honk, that's what."

Susie turned into her driveway, her steps slowing as she fumbled for her key. Even after three years, she hated coming home to an empty house. It had seemed emptier after Nora went back to work, as if something had gone out of the warm family feeling in the comfortable rooms.

Reminding herself of the park party, she felt a rise of anticipation dissipate the chill within her. Of course, they weren't really parties. The crowd just gathered, singly or in couples, about twenty kids from the neighborhood.

Most of them had known each other since kindergarten. Meeting at the little park, they danced on the shuffleboard area and talked and laughed and had fun. It *was* fun, and what was so awful about a few drinks? Mark had been a real pain about it. Small loss, he was.

The house was cold, shut tightly all day against the warmth outside. Susie turned up the thermostat and headed for the kitchen, hungry and thirsty. For hours she had been looking forward to cheese and crackers with a beer. But just as she reached for a cold frosty can, she heard Casey's car in the drive, so she took a Coke instead.

That was one thing about Friday afternoons. Casey usually came home early. Most people were too busy to talk to him, he said, or they knocked off early, too.

When he came in the back door, Susie was sitting at the table, slicing cheese.

"Hi, Suse. Great day to play hookey," he said amiably. "Were you tempted?"

She eyed him. "The thought never crossed my mind. You know what a strong character I have."

His eyes twinkled. "Yeah. Well, a day like this must have been a real test." He opened the refrigerator, reappeared a moment later around the door with a can of beer in his hand.

Susie watched him peel the little metal tab back, flip it on the counter, and lift the can to drink deeply. Her mouth watered. She could almost taste the fizzy brew, the first swallow that made your tongue prickle as it slid by.

He lowered the can, eyes sober as he looked at her, his gaze speculative. "Going out tonight?"

She felt anger rise in a hot surge through her chest. Always reading her mind, damn him, always reading her as if he had some kind of weird X-ray in his head right behind those bright-blue eyes.

Her throat too dry to speak normally, to even try to pretend he hadn't hit target, she nodded and reached for a cracker so she wouldn't have to look at him.

A short silence.

Then he sighed, sat down at the table, helped himself to a cracker and a piece of cheese. "Down at the park?"

Susie looked at him. She wanted to say something cold and sarcastic, something like, "Any objections?" But she couldn't. No matter how she felt about him, she just couldn't bring herself to cut him. That was crazy in a way because she spent hours in silent dialogue, really telling him off, but she never said a word aloud that came close to the things she might be thinking.

"Why?"

He shrugged. "Seemed a nice night for it. La Dawn going, too?"

She nodded, thinking irritably, now a game of twenty questions?

Both Casey and Nora loved La Dawn. Sometimes Susie felt a vague annoyance about that, especially when they held her up as a shining example. But then she'd feel ashamed of herself. La Dawn was something special, and if Casey could see that, well, chalk up one small point for Mr. Wonderful.

Susie fixed herself a plate of snacks and took off for her room, but taking her time about it so it wouldn't look as if she were cutting him off. She said to herself scornfully, *Can't be rude about it. Can't hurt his feelings, can we?*

As she closed the door of her room, it swept over her again, an aching feeling of unhappiness. She felt as if she were changing into something totally alien to the person she used to be. She didn't like this new Susie, quick to anger, at odds with almost everyone. The slow, inexorable change frightened her as well because she couldn't seem to stop the process.

She sometimes thought, in bleak despair, that she would end up trapped inside a personality she detested, unable to communicate with the people she truly loved.

What was happening to her?

Quickly, she grasped at the one remedy she had discovered which could diminish the pain. Only a few hours more and she could leave for the park. A couple of drinks would take away all the hurt, dissolve the cold knot of fear in her stomach. After a few drinks, everything would be fine.

CHAPTER
THREE

It was after six by the time La Dawn crossed the glassed-in porch at the front of her home and opened the inner door. She thought crossly, of all nights for Miss Chaney to ask how she liked her new part-time job, she had to pick Friday.

She sighed as she dumped her books and jacket on the hall table. Actually, she liked Miss Chaney and knew the feeling was mutual. If only their discussion had been postponed until a weekday! Tony would be here at 7:30, and she had to shower and sew a button on her plaid pantsuit and —

Her mother called from the dining room, "La Dawn, is that you?"

"Last time I looked, I was me." She stuck her head around the door. "Mom, honestly, I don't have time to eat. Miss Chaney kept me talking and I have to — "

Valadia Holland shook her head, but her eyes were soft with indulgent amusement. "Take you longer than an hour to get beautiful?"

Twelve-year-old Jay snorted. "Tony better get set for a long wait. Like till nine o'clock, maybe."

His father glanced at him, and Jay bent over his plate again, giggling.

Monrovia Taylor wiggled in his chair. At five, he was a rounded cherub with a happy disposition. But now he slumped, small chin resting on the table. "All through eating," he announced, the words issuing from his propped jaws with a strained ponderous sound. "My teeth are tired."

His mother looked at his empty plate. "I'm not surprised," she said mildly. Then, to her daughter, "Run along. I'll bring you a milk-shake."

"Thanks, Mom!" Startled and pleased, La Dawn hurried up the stairs. She hadn't really expected her mother to let her skip dinner, the one meal the whole family shared. Her father left early in the morning for his job in the city. So the rule about sitting down to the evening meal was never easily broached.

By the time she emerged from the shower, she heard a tap at the door. Wrapped in her towel, La Dawn went to take the tall glass.

"Strawberry! Yum. You are my very favorite lady."

"Flattery will get you — some peanut cookies, too." Her mother reached in her apron pocket for the cookies wrapped in a napkin. "I'm assuming Tony will feed you a hamburger sometime during the evening. If he doesn't, you better get a bite before you go to bed. Your breakfasts sure don't amount to much these days."

La Dawn grinned. "And I'm just a growing girl, right? The way my mama's always shoving groceries at me, I'm going to be growing horizontally."

Her mother waved the words aside. "Nobody in this family is carrying an extra ounce. Oh, maybe Monrovia Taylor is, but that's just baby fat. Way he runs from morning till night, I don't know how he holds onto it, and that's a fact."

She reached for the doorknob to pull the door shut. "Get some clothes on before you catch your death."

La Dawn got into her woolly robe and sat on the edge of her bed to sew on the button, reaching from time to time to sip from the glass on her bed table. It was a nice comfortable thing, she reflected, to have parents you loved, and to feel understanding grow as you got older.

Her father had gone to night school for years, working long hard hours for his present job as a C.P.A. with Commonwealth Edison.

"C.P.A. That stands for Cotton Pickin' Accountant," he'd say, winking at the kids.

His wife never failed to take the bait, explaining what a Certified Public Accountant was and that it was like getting a degree. You had to take an exam before you were certified, and lots of people couldn't pass it.

"We're almost as smart as those folks who work down at the motor vehicle place," Hal Holland would say, teasing his wife about her job, amusement on his long thin face. "You got to have your brains in high gear, puttin' in a day's work down there."

"Now, Hal, you stop that! These children have a right to be proud of their daddy. Can't tell them too many times how hard you worked for everything we got."

About that time he'd grab her and nuzzle her neck where she was so ticklish, and she'd scream with laughter. All the kids got the message, that they were proud of each other along with loving each other. There seemed to be enough of that feeling to spill over onto La Dawn and her little brothers.

A hamburger, her mother had said, and La Dawn felt a twinge of guilt. Though she had never lied to her parents about what went on at the park parties, they hadn't asked a straight-out question for a long time.

"Never any drugs, are there?" her father had asked last year when the park parties first became popular.

"No, Daddy."

"Liquor? Hard stuff?"

La Dawn told him honestly, "Not very often. A couple of the boys bring it once in a while. But there's never been any trouble. And you know I don't like it. I take a sip of your beer in the summer sometimes, but I never want more than that."

It was still true. She could nurse a beer all evening long. If one of the kids hassled her about it, she just made some wise remark about saving herself for the really heavy vices.

She had told Susie once, firmly and without a smile, "Look, if it's all the same to you, I like to feel I'm playing with a full deck, okay?"

La Dawn sighed as she cut the thread and put her sewing kit aside. Her thoughts followed a familiar pattern while she dressed, then sat down to fix her face and hair at the little dressing table that had been a gift for her tenth birthday.

Susie. Something had to be done about Susie. But how could she get through to her about her drinking without turning her off? How? She had said as much as she dared, backing off quickly when she saw her friend bristle, flaring irritably as she did so often these days.

If only there were someone she could talk to about Susie. Absently, La Dawn dabbed perfume on her wrists and throat, then paused to wonder if she had already done that. She'd have to check with her mother to make sure she didn't send Tony into shock.

No, she thought, there wasn't anyone she could consult about Susie's problem, not without a lot of static from guidance counselors and other well-meaning types who would insist on names and facts. A dozen times she had agonized over every possible course of action, only to come to the same dead end.

She and Tony seemed to be the only ones in the crowd concerned about Susie. Well, Mark had been, but he certainly hadn't handled the situation with any cool whatsoever. He was just scared out of his skull that Susie would get into some kind of trouble, and he might be involved, too.

Susie desperately needed friends now. La Dawn enlarged on that thought and made a face at the mirror as she studied her eye make-up. Susie needed people who not only would see that she was going through a mixed-up phase, but who would understand why — people who cared about her enough to help. La Dawn was really frightened, suspecting that Susie was heading for the kind of bad time that none of them could cope with, not her friends, not her parents, maybe not anybody.

Nora Sears was a sweet lady, La Dawn thought, but one with a big blind spot where Susie was concerned. Whereas that very classy dude, Mr. Casey Sears, had Susie's number from his first week on the scene. That was part of the problem, of course.

The last thing Susie wanted was somebody

trying to take her father's place, which Casey wasn't trying to do. Someone who knew the score so well, he added her up on the first look. Casey could be the best thing that had happened to Susie since her father died, if she gave him half a chance. But she wouldn't — until it was too late, probably.

La Dawn shook her head as if that would dispose of the depressing thoughts that weighed upon her. She tied a matching plaid scarf around her hair, trying to arrange it so it looked the way it did on the cute model in *Co-Ed*, studying it in her hand mirror from all angles. It didn't look as glamorous as it did in the magazine, but chances were, that model chick had lots of help with hers.

Well, that model wouldn't have anybody as great as Tony to try it out on. La Dawn turned from the mirror, satisfied. Tony was strictly one of a kind. Beautiful, that man. It had been a day for the history books when the Johnsons moved on this block.

She opened the door and heard a rush of voices from the downstairs hall. Her little brothers swarmed all over Tony when he came to pick her up, but Tony was cool. He had little brothers himself.

Running down the stairs, she felt the swelling happiness within, the eagerness, the excitement about the evening ahead — maybe four full hours with him. It couldn't be more than that — she wouldn't let it be more than that

— because Tony had to be up early to open the Standard station his father managed on Main Street.

He grinned at her, looking up from a boxing crouch, fists cocked as Jay circled him. From a seat on his shoulders, Monrovia Taylor laughed shrilly, fingers buried in Tony's afro.

"Monrovia Taylor Holland, you're getting too big to ride piggy-back. What did Mama tell you about that?"

Tony swung the small boy to the floor. "It's not his weight that bothers me," he said and did a bug-eyed Flip Wilson take. "He's messin' up ma hairdo!"

A few minutes later they approached the park, strolling over the Japanese bridge hand-in-hand, already hearing the faint music from two or three transistors. As they came around the tennis courts they could see several couples dancing in the shuffleboard area. Pam and Scott. Mark and his new girl, someone named Diane. Susie and — who was Susie with?

La Dawn frowned. Greg Livingston? Oh, not Greg. It wasn't that Susie didn't know exactly what it was with him. Greg was one bad dude, strictly Mr. Trouble. But Susie with a couple of drinks — or four or five, more likely — now *that* Susie wouldn't care a whole lot.

Tony read her mind, something he did with amazing ease. Squeezing her hand, he leaned close to say softly, reassuringly, "Now, we can take her home when we leave. Come on, babe, no more worrying. We're here to have fun. Right?"

"Sure, Tony. Sure." She reached up to kiss him. What he was, was great, that's all. Sometimes she wondered how she'd been lucky enough to interest Tony Johnson. He could have any girl he wanted.

"Hey, La Dawn! Tony!"

Susie ran to greet them, eyes shining, cheeks flushed, lovely in an emerald green pantsuit, a marvelous color with her red hair. But La Dawn could tell from the way she looked and from her breezy manner that she'd already been hitting something. Greg always had some booze with him, of course. But if Susie would get cozy with someone like Greg just because of that, she was in bigger trouble than La Dawn had feared.

She tried to play it with a light touch. "Susie, you bozo!" It had always been her affectionate name for her friend. "You dance like that with the wolfman, you come home at dawn with bites on your neck."

Susie giggled. "I can handle him. Oh, listen, that's David Bowic! Come on, let's get this party off the ground."

La Dawn saw her dancing with three or four boys in succession, her laughter frequently cutting through the sound of voices and music. Guilty about dividing her attention, La Dawn concentrated wholly on Tony for the next hour or two.

When she looked for Susie again, she couldn't see her anywhere. Bumping into Pam in the rest room, she grabbed her arm.

"Have you seen Susie?"

Pam laughed. "Greg's opened the bar in the back of his car. I suppose that's where she is." She wrinkled her nose. "I can't understand her *liking* the stuff. I couldn't get it down if they didn't put it in orange crush — or maybe strawberry wine."

La Dawn let her go, thinking gloomily that Pam didn't realize she might be luckier than Susie. The first time Susie had had a drink, she had insisted it was great, really great. La Dawn recalled laughing to herself, thinking it was a put-on. Vodka was like the strongest cough medicine ever, and it hit your stomach like liquid fire. Nobody could really enjoy stuff like that. But now, she wondered.

As she feared, Susie was not about to leave the party at eleven o'clock or eleven-fifteen or even eleven-thirty.

"Go 'way!" she chortled, her eyes feverishly bright. "Away with all party poopers!"

La Dawn turned away silently, knowing that Tony would stay if she asked him, losing an hour of sleep he'd regret in the morning. But she knew, as well, that it wouldn't do any good. Susie wouldn't go home as long as the bar was open in the back of Greg Livingston's car.

CHAPTER
FOUR

Susie quickly shut her eyes against the painful glare from the sun streaming through the windows. She came awake slowly, taking inventory. Her mouth tasted horrible, and her head vibrated with a slow, heavy pounding.

Cautiously, she raised it from the pillow a few inches, then lowered it with a soft moan. Her stomach seemed to be taking orders from upstairs, and the message from her aching head was loud and irritable: We're all in this together. Don't think you're going to get off without a few problems.

Wow. The Granddaddy of all hangovers. It took several minutes for Susie to struggle upright in bed, then slowly swing her legs over the edge. She held her head in her hands for a moment, vaguely surprised that her fingers couldn't detect the pulsing throb that made it feel as if it might come loose from her shoulders.

That must have been some party last night. She squeezed her eyes shut again, trying to remember. Well, it had been really neat at first. Crazy guys like DeHaven, Tim, and Greg smuggling in the six packs and a bottle or two. Tim and DeHaven had drawn watch-for-the-cops duty, one hour on and one hour off, and they both concentrated on her when they came back to the party.

She had come to life with the old excitement, laughing and dancing, at ease with herself as she always was after a few drinks. It was such a great feeling, as if she were the prettiest, most popular girl there, all square with the world, loving everybody — oh, with a few minor exceptions, maybe. Like Mark, for instance, who looked at her reproachfully every time they bumped into each other.

She hadn't seen too much of La Dawn and Tony. She seemed to have a vague recollection that they had wanted to take her home early. Too bad they always had to miss the best part of the evening because Tony had to open the station every morning. Well, La Dawn didn't like to drink, anyway.

Pam was sure a good sport, though. She didn't like the taste any more than La Dawn did, but she drank it in orange crush or something like that. Most of the kids didn't care too much about mixing the stuff with pills. DeHaven and Tim did, though, and they'd go on and on about the super high that could give you.

Something on the edge of her thoughts kept nagging at her. Susie frowned, then regretted even that slight movement of her forehead. Something — what was it? Coming home? But she couldn't remember coming home, not much about it, anyway. Still, no matter how much she had to drink, she always seemed to collect herself by the time she reached her door.

She recalled tiptoeing upstairs. It had been quite late, long after the curfew hour Nora had set for her. And she knocked the hairdryer onto the bathroom floor. That really helped clear her head because she was scared the racket had awakened her mother.

After that, she crawled into bed. And now it was nine o'clock, and she wouldn't be awake yet except for having to go to the bathroom. So what was it that kept picking at her about last night? What was it she couldn't remember?

In the bathroom she carefully splashed cold water on her face and drank thirstily from her cupped hands. Then it came back; a few flashes, anyway, giving her enough of a clue so that she hastily pushed it away in that dark closet of her memory where it had been hiding.

Greg Livingston. He had brought her home. And what had happened? No, far better not to try to fill in those blank hours. Better to take a shower and think about something else. Yes, a shower would help. Warm water, soothing warm water and soap — oceans of soap —

Afterward, she was just wriggling into her robe, shivering because the house wasn't too warm yet, when her mother tapped on the door.

"Susie? I want to talk to you."

Susie froze, hearing something in Nora's voice that alerted her to trouble. So she had heard her come in last night. That must be it.

Susie put on a smile as she opened the door. "I know, I know," she said lightly, "it was way too late last night. I told Greg I'd catch it this morning. Such a gorgeous night, he insisted we go for a drive. He's like a little kid, driving that big car of his dad's.

"Then the darned thing blew a tire. Oh, it was a rear one, no trouble getting off the road. Only old hotshot Greg discovered the spare had a slow leak, and it wasn't any good, either. Thing was, his dad told him weeks ago to get that tire fixed."

She laughed, a pretty good laugh considering she was getting uncomfortably deep into the world of fiction. "So at least I can find a little comfort in the fact that Greg's getting chewed out, too, along about this time — "

As she talked, Nora's small face relaxed. She sighed and shook her head, but her eyes said she'd bought the story. Her eyes said she knew it had been something like that.

"You should have called. Casey could have

gone to help. It's not safe, honey, on the high-way late at night."

Susie's painful twinge of guilt and shame diminished with the mention of Casey's name. Mr. Wonderful to the rescue. Sure. And after the third degree and a little breath-sampling session, he would have huffed and puffed and blown that tire up all by himself. If there had been a flat tire in the first place.

As Nora went down the hall, Susie leaned against the door frame watching her, holding a little desperately to her irritation with Casey. If she kept that on the front burner, reminding herself why she had every reason to be mad at the big clown, then — then maybe she wouldn't go back to what her mother had said.

"It's not safe, honey, on the highway late at night."

Down in the kitchen Casey was speaking to her mother so emphatically that every word reached the upstairs hall.

"Nora, baby, listen to me. This kid has a problem, and you've got to face it. She needs help, not a couple of parents who brush this sort of thing off as a few wild oats in the breeze."

Susie crept to the head of the stairs and sat on the top step, listening intently.

Her mother retorted in a voice husky with anger. Susie pictured her, head back, chin high, eyes flashing as she spoke.

"You're the one who doesn't understand,

Casey. And I don't appreciate your coming on like the proverbial heavy stepfather. Especially over a misunderstanding."

A short silence.

"You don't believe what the police are trying to get across to the schools and the community about the kind of drinking these kids are into?"

"Come on, Casey! Don't you remember how it was a few years ago with half of them on drugs? Well, if you've forgotten, I haven't. I saw too many of them in the emergency room. We *lost* too many of them there."

"Nora — "

"No, you listen to *me*! She's my daughter. Are you trying to say I don't know my own daughter? And those kids down at the park last night, I've known most of them, too, since they were in diapers. They're good kids!"

Casey said something so quietly Susie had to strain to hear. "Those good kids are experimenting with something just as dangerous as pills and — honey, you're a nurse. You're well aware of something a lot of people never think about. Liquor is a drug."

Nora slammed something into the sink. But she sounded merely weary of the argument. "At least it's legal. And you're right. It is something I know about, something that doesn't scare me like those damned pills and heroin and all the stuff they sniff to get high.

"Look, I went to parties when I was sixteen, and the boys spiked the punch. Or they carried flasks so they could sneak a shot in the Cokes when nobody was looking. In fact, the wildest kid in our bunch — Dick Ballantyne, his name was — do you know where he is now?"

She laughed, a high-pitched brittle sound. "He's an officer in the Trust Department of the First National Bank."

"You know something?" Casey sounded not only tired, but defeated. "Your old buddy Ballantyne was lucky. Or maybe he was smart enough to get into the AA program somewhere along the line. These kids we're talking about, Nora, if they get drunk as often as I have a hunch they do, they'll turn into kids who need booze to function normally. And you know as well as I do what they turn into after that."

Nora's voice was muffled, as if she had walked into the pantry off the kitchen. "I don't want to argue about it any more. I won't convince you of anything, and you sure aren't going to make any points, either. Because I know those kids. And I trust them — trust Susie with them — to a certain extent, naturally. I'm not that naïve. I want to know who she's with and I won't put up with any nonsense about her breaking the house rules."

"There was some good reason then for the hour she got in last night?"

"As a matter of fact, there was. Greg Livingston took her for a drive, had a blowout, and the spare tire was flat, too."

Nora laughed. "I know. It's the oldest story

going, next to the one about running out of gas. So I'm sure it must be the truth. Susie could come up with a better fib than that if she really wanted to put one over."

The back door opened, and Casey's voice rumbled from the porch for a moment before the door closed again. Susie heard water running in the sink, the clatter of dishes being stacked on the drainboard.

Abruptly she became aware of herself, still crouched in a listening posture, head pressed against the bannister, like a little kid trying to hear what the grown-ups downstairs were talking about.

Well, little kids didn't know any better. When somebody her age eavesdropped, they didn't have any such excuse. There was no reason to feel good about selling that dumb story to Nora, either. Her mother trusted her, and this wasn't the first time she had traded on that knowledge.

Before the hurt from that thought became unbearable, she pushed it away. If Nora hadn't married Casey, this sort of thing wouldn't be happening. All right, she'd been lonely. Now she wasn't alone any more. She had him.

Susie got to her feet slowly, thinking, who does that leave me? Nobody. Well, at least she knew Casey for the enemy now. She had suspected for a long time that he was wise to the park parties. Now the little exchange between him and her mother had confirmed it.

She caught a wisp of the aroma from frying bacon and felt her stomach squirm. Retreating quickly to the bathroom, she locked the door and leaned against it for moment, her eyes closed.

Nora would handle Casey, all right. Even if she couldn't, the first priority now was something for this thundering headache. Down on her knees, she reached for the alcohol container under the sink. Then, sitting with her forehead against the cool tile wall, she swigged the vodka she had put in the bottle a week ago.

Never again, she thought. She'd never overdo it like that again.

CHAPTER
FIVE

Two weeks later at the breakfast table, Casey quoted blithely, " 'And what is so rare as a day in June — ?' " finishing in his own words, "A warm sunny day in June in the suburbs of Chicago. Enjoy it, girls, because it won't last. Weatherman says there's a storm moving in. The sun may not shine again until July."

"That's a cheery thought," Nora said, and reached for his cup. "More coffee?"

Susie said nothing, very much aware of her own personal stormclouds gathering overhead. Report cards were due today, and she was suffering through the last stages of a drippy cold. One of those twin miseries would have been enough to ruin the nicest day in the year. Two of them assured a dismal forecast.

"Isn't today the day you get your grades?"

her mother inquired, adding the final gloomy touch.

Susie had been hoping she would forget. Oh, well, why prolong the agony? she thought. It would be bad enough getting the news today. Why sweat out the eventual heavy scene when her mother saw the card?

"They're not going to be so great." She made a face and sipped her orange juice, not looking at her mother. Maybe she could come down with a speedy case of pneumonia, and Nora would forget her awful grades in a dramatic rush to the hospital.

"Oh, Susie. Are you going to have to go to summer school?"

Susie's head jerked up. "No way will I go to summer school," she said flatly. "I didn't say I was flunking anything. Even if I did, you couldn't drag me back to summer classes. I have had it with school and dumb teachers and stuff like grammar and math. I detest grammar and math." The last words emerged through clenched teeth.

Nora sighed. "Well, if you plan on being a doctor, you haven't seen anything like what they're going to throw at you in college. Really tough science classes, labs — you'll be reading stacks of books until your eyes won't focus. And there will always be another stack waiting for you."

Susie looked at her and slowly shook her head. "Mom, I never said I planned on being a doctor. You're the one who keeps saying it."

Nora threw out her hands. "But that's crazy! Now's the time for women to go into medicine. You don't have to be a nurse any more. You have a choice!"

"You're probably right." Susie took a deep breath. She felt just miserable enough to dish out some unpleasant truths for a change. "There's one thing you keep overlooking, as if it might change or go away if you ignore it. Mom, I don't have doctor-type brains."

Casey cleared his throat, but when she turned to look at him, he was buttering his toast, no expression on his face.

"Don't be silly." Nora brushed her words away with a short erasing gesture. "You just aren't motivated to use the brains you've got, that's all. And I can't imagine why. I *desperately* wanted to be a doctor, and I had to settle for the only field where I had a chance. I mean, it's a long haul. I didn't have any family to back me financially or any other way. But you do."

Angry words boiled up inside Susie. She pressed her lips together hard. They might pop out otherwise, and she knew if she said even part of what she was thinking she'd regret it.

Cool it, she thought. There would be enough flak about her grades without needling Nora on a sensitive point right now. After a moment she took her plate to the sink and rinsed it with great care, aware of the heavy silence behind her.

With an effort she made her voice casual as she picked up her thermos and lunch sack from the sink and turned to smile at her mother.

"See you tonight," she said, "if I'm not in intensive care by then."

"All right, dear." Nora still looked troubled, but her voice sounded normal, if a little pre-occupied.

Susie made a quick trip upstairs to get a sweater, just in case the weatherman was right about that storm moving in. She filled the thermos, already three-quarters full of orange juice, with a generous amount of vodka from the supply in her bathroom cabinet. That should knock her head cold, she thought, as she snapped the lid back in place.

As she hurried down the stairs, Casey came out in the hall. She just had time to tuck the thermos inside her sweater.

"Susie, I want you to know I think you're wise to give some thought to the job you want. And now's the time to do it." He leaned against the wall beside the antique table that Nora loved. Every Saturday she polished it until it shone, and then cleaned the silver bowl that was exactly centered on the gleaming surface.

"The people who love you try to advise you," he went on, "but it's up to you to make up your own mind. You may be working at the same job for years, off and on, for half your life.

Nobody knows about something like that. So make sure it's something you like doing, something you're good at."

He grinned at her, the tough-little-boy grin that amused her even when she was trying to be mad at him. "If you get confused about what people tell you you'll be good at, remember this. *My* folks wanted me to be a minister."

Susie stared at him. Standing on the bottom step, she had been waiting impatiently for him to get to the point, so the punch line almost got past her.

Then it echoed again between them, and she burst out laughing. "You? A minister? You never should have told me, Casey. From now on, no matter what you're saying, I'll picture you in the pulpit!"

He chuckled and shrugged one bulky shoulder. "You could be picturing me in worse places."

All the way to school, Susie kept thinking of what he had said, giggling to herself about anybody considering Casey a candidate for the ministry, even a brace of doting parents. She had to walk alone today. Pam had been to the dentist to have two wisdom teeth pulled, and La Dawn was on the early shift at the library this week.

It was a funny thing, Susie mused, the business of picking out a career. When you were little you assumed you could be anything you wanted to be, as if somebody would wave a magic wand one day and — zap! — instant movie star or tennis champ or Mother of the Year or whatever you thought was really neat.

When she and La Dawn and Pam were much younger it had been a favorite game they played on long, dull, rainy afternoons, projecting themselves into fascinating futures.

Pam had lacked imagination to go much further than, "A model, maybe? For hair or shoes or something. I'd never be skinny enough for clothes."

She had glanced ruefully at her rounded stomach and chubby legs. "I used to think I'd be an actress, but I guess they work awfully hard, and they're always on horrible diets. Mom said the camera makes you look twenty pounds fatter. Isn't that gross?"

La Dawn gave the matter serious consideration. Lying on her bed with Brotherbear, the battered little black and brown panda perched on one knee, she talked directly to him.

"Hey, there, Brothuh! A jive job, the first time a black woman ever does — what? No, there's already a Congresswoman and movie stars and singers and models — "

"So how about being a really famous writer?" Susie raised her head from the pillow of the opposite bed. "I know, there are lots of black women writers. But I mean somebody so famous, you'd win the Bulitzer Prize and — "

"*Pulitzer!*" La Dawn said, outraged. "You bozo!"

But she was intrigued by the idea. Anybody could see that. She started carrying little notebooks and writing in a journal, not a diary. That was kid stuff, she said, for recording who sat next to you in school and what you had for lunch that day.

Journals were for writing your thoughts and feelings or for poetry or for describing something like a sunset, so utterly beautiful you looked at it and wanted to cry.

As for Susie, she had decided early on a career in medicine, not surprising for the daughter of a doctor and a nurse. But it was something entirely different from the career her mother envisioned for her.

"I'm going to be someone like Florence Nightingale," she stated confidently during that long-ago discussion. "Or like Dr. Salk. I mean, I'll do something really great, curing an epidemic all by myself, maybe. And hundreds of people will be so grateful they'll line up to kiss my hand."

"Sounds awfully germy to me," La Dawn drawled, "for a Florence Nightingale type." She sat up to grin at Susie and toss Brotherbear over to rest on the opposite pillow.

Susie smiled, remembering. Not so long ago La Dawn had also recalled that day, teasing her about it. "Way I see it, bozo, you got two options. Go for the nurse's cap. Or if you do end up hanging out your shingle, marry a lawyer. One who specializes in malpractice cases."

Susie walked slowly along the locker corridor, paying no attention to the students hurrying by, bumping into her and pushing her aside in their rush to get to the first class of the day. Even though she was late herself, she took her time pawing through the assortment of books and notebooks on her locker shelf.

Why hurry when you were locked into the same rut in the middle of a treadmill? Where was she going? Nowhere. Not to any dedicated life as somebody like Florence Nightingale or Dr. Salk, that was for sure. With the grade coming up in biology, she could forget a career in science, any kind of science.

The first bell rang, echoing through the hall now empty of all but one or two stragglers. Susie leaned her head against the cold metal locker door, feeling lost and alone and chilled to the bone with fear. What was going to become of her? Why was she isolated from everybody, even the people she loved best?

There was nobody in the whole world who could understand, tell her what was wrong, what she was doing that inevitably made a mess of things in her life.

On the point of slamming the door shut, she reached for her thermos, poured a half cup of juice and vodka and drank it quickly. She hadn't remembered to shake it up very well, and the liquor gave her a warm glow by the time she reached the office for her tardy pass.

She was feeling a little better at the end of second period, though her grades were as bad as she expected they would be. Then Miss Emerson, the biology teacher, beckoned to her as she headed for the door. Susie waited, but the teacher didn't speak until the room was empty.

"Susie, you're capable of better work. You should have had a much higher grade." Miss Emerson smiled, and her small face warmed, looking almost pretty for a moment. She was a petite young woman, smaller-boned and even more fragile than Nora.

"I just wanted to tell you that I've been concerned about you. I wanted you to know that — well, if anything is wrong — if there's some way I can help — I would be so glad if you'd ask — " Her voice dwindled in the absence of any response.

Susie looked at her, keeping her face blank. When she spoke, her voice was quiet, polite, a little puzzled. "Oh, no, there's nothing wrong. Maybe I just have spring fever. I just — sort of — lost interest."

"Oh." The small face flushed, tightened as her smile disappeared. "Well, I just thought I'd ask. You seemed so interested the first few weeks, so full of questions and — I'm sorry. I didn't mean to pry. I just thought I'd ask — "

She turned away and after a moment Susie

walked out, unhurriedly, so the teacher would know for sure that she'd made a mistake. Still, it was unreal how one painfully shy, solemn-faced little teacher like Miss Emerson could see something wrong and make an effort — it obviously had been difficult for her — to reach out and communicate. Yes, that was the word, though it was one Susie disliked. People used it so much, it didn't seem to mean much any more.

Out in the hall, she paused a few feet from the door. Maybe if she went back and tried to explain — No, how could she explain something she didn't understand herself? How could Miss Emerson help when Nora couldn't or La Dawn or — no, better leave it the way it was. Besides, Miss Emerson had just given her a D in biology, hadn't she? Nora was going to have a fit about that.

Susie walked on down the hall. If she hurried, she'd have time to go by her locker for a short drink. That should hold her until lunchtime.

CHAPTER
SIX

School let out at noon on the last day, and Susie took her time cleaning out her locker. There wasn't any reason to hurry, she thought, with a strange empty feeling inside. Absently, she bundled grubby tennis shoes and even grubbier white socks inside her clean gym suit.

After today there wouldn't be much to look forward to. Not that she was crazy about school, but it did fill the days, and it was fun seeing her friends in class. Now, the summer stretched ahead in a tremendous scary vacuum. A lot of the girls, like La Dawn, had jobs, or else they were busy with boyfriends in their spare time.

She didn't have anyone special any more, despite Greg Livingston's possessive attitude of late. He had a big mouth, too, Susie thought, frowning. She knew he was spreading a lot of stories, because some of them had gotten back to her. If only he weren't such a handy source for buying an occasional bottle.

She had decided weeks ago to cool it with Greg, to make sure she wasn't alone with him again. The minute she found another way to buy, well, it would be a happy day when she could tell him exactly what she thought of him.

Still, without Greg, it would be a real drag buying a bottle. Some of the kids just hung around a liquor store asking the customers to buy for them, but that could be a hassle, too. Sometimes people got really nasty about it. Susie had never dared try that method, however. Even across town in another neighborhood, it would be just her luck to run into one of her mother's friends.

La Dawn came hurrying down the hall at that moment, pausing to grin at Susie over the huge pile of books, sweaters, and gym clothes she was carrying.

"Hey, bozo, how about coming for dinner and to spend the night. You and Pam. I'm getting off early, so you could come over about five. We can celebrate the last day of school. Okay?"

"Sure, that'd be great. You and Tony don't have anything planned?"

"I told him he'll have to wait till Saturday. Tonight's just for girls. And he said — " There was a sparkle of amusement in her dark eyes.

"Well, never mind what he said. But I told him I'm worth waiting for, and the man never argues that point."

She waved awkwardly with the hand clutching the laces to her gym shoes, then hurried on.

Susie felt her spirits rise. There would be something fun to anticipate for tonight, anyway. It had been cool and rainy all week. Nobody would plan a park party in this kind of weather. No one had mentioned any other kind of party, either, so that meant all the parents were staying home tonight, too. Well, that was okay. A chaperoned affair wasn't all that much fun. With nothing on hand but Cokes and chips and dip, forget it.

She stacked her books on the floor with the bundle of gym clothes on top, then looked down the crowded aisle for Pam. No sense standing around holding all this stuff if she had to wait five minutes for Pam to get it in gear. But she saw her friend heading in her direction, books balanced on one hip.

"Where's your gym stuff?"

"Home." Pam giggled. "I've been excused all week. I said I'd hurt my ankle."

Susie had to laugh. "Someone's sure to check up on you."

Pam said cheerfully, "I'd tell the truth if they did. I just hate swimming and going around reeking of chlorine the rest of the day. Besides, the worst they ever do is give you make-up classes. You can do that after school."

With a groan, Susie lifted her books and followed Pam to the door. "It's not worth it," she said. "Once they peg you for a sharpie, they never believe anything after that."

In the echo of her own words, she felt a wave of self-contempt. Listen to the authority on how and when to tell the truth, she thought. When had she changed into the kind of person who figured there was a good reason for a certain kind of lie, to certain people? To Nora, for instance, because Nora would never believe that she had learned to lie skillfully and easily.

She began to chatter to Pam, pushing back the knife-sharp accusing thoughts, the vivid pictures of a second Susie, the one she had begun to fear as well as despise.

"Did La Dawn ask you to come tonight — for dinner and to sleep over? Can you talk Scott into doing without you for one night? Please do, Pam. It's been forever since we've been together, just the three of us."

"No problem." Pam swung her long blonde hair over one shoulder. "My mother says Scott and I have been seeing too much of each other. In fact, she's making noises about cutting us down to a couple afternoons and evenings a week. I mean, now that summer's coming on."

Susie peered at the gray sky, black rain-clouds building up in the east. "Summer! We get about six weeks that are hot and horrible, two or three weeks that are really nice, and that'll be it." She smiled at Pam. "But it's neat that you can come tonight."

"You know what I want us to talk about?" Pam's gray eyes widened eagerly. "Summer jobs. If I can't see Scott as much as I'd like, the time's going to drag something awful. And think of the clothes I could buy for next year!"

Susie nodded. She knew La Dawn was saving her money for college. The Hollands would have a problem helping three kids through school. Susie wasn't all that excited about college herself, but she liked the idea of a new wardrobe. And of not being home alone.

No, it wouldn't be so great being tempted by the booze in the house, for one thing. Especially now that she knew Casey was on to her. He'd zero in the first time she got caught raiding the liquor cabinet. What a hassle that would be!

When she told Nora her plans for the evening, her mother was delighted. "Let me send that recipe for carrot bread down to Valadia. I've been promising for weeks to write it out for her."

She gave Susie the slip of paper as she was going out the door. "You girls have a good visit now. It's been a long time since you got together like this. I've been thinking that — well, honey, you've been partying too much."

As if she regretted the hint of reproach in her words, she patted her daughter's arm. "You've got time enough ahead of you for that, heaven knows. Take advantage of the fun you can have now with good friends like La Dawn and Pam. All too soon, you'll be going your separate ways, working or off to different schools. And then you'll be sorry you missed the sort of thing you can be doing right now. This is a very special time in your life."

Susie heard the wistful note in her mother's voice, and for a fleeting moment, she felt really close to her, the way they had been in the years before Casey came along. At the same time, she felt something akin to pity for her mother. Nora seemed to have such a fierce need to know that this sixteenth year was wonderful in every way for her daughter. But how could she help seeing that daughter had never been more miserable?

Susie hardened herself against the impulse to throw herself in Nora's arms, to cry on her shoulder. Her hands tightened on the handle of her overnight bag.

What would she say, anyway? *Look at me! Care about me! Help me!* No, there wasn't room for her in Nora's life any more, not for any of her problems. The way her mother must figure, she had given her daughter all her time and attention during the years up until now — and it was somebody else's turn. It was Casey's turn.

Susie walked down the street toward Pam's house, deep in thought. She barely responded to her friend's non-stop monologue, the warm laughing voice going on and on in an endless breathless stream of words.

Inside La Dawn's house she made an effort to shrug off the gray mood. She greeted Monrovia Taylor with unfeigned delight. To her, he had always been one of the world's most fantastic kids. It was not merely that he was cuddly and cute looking. He was extraordinary in a dozen different ways; unspoiled, bright, and possessed of a way of saying things with a kind of reverse English so that they came out unexpectedly funny, or colored with unique insight.

Susie treasured moments like the one a few weeks ago when he had brought her his mother's carnation corsage to smell.

"I can't smell it, love," she told him. "I have a cold."

Monrovia Taylor looked from her to the flower, thoughtfully, and again he drew a cockeyed conclusion. "Will the flower catch your cold?"

Now, he steered Susie to a chair and, one by one, brought her his kindergarten projects, crayoned pictures, fingerpaintings, and a rather lumpy, lopsided, clay ashtray.

"That's for my daddy."

"But your daddy doesn't smoke."

"I know." He shrugged. "But the other stuff was blotters and pencil-holders. The other stuff was dumb."

Susie nodded. "Well, for your first shot at

an ashtray, I have to say it's sensational."

He always seemed to appreciate her honesty.

From the arm of her chair the small boy confided, "It's not the way an ashtray should be. But until I did it, you know, I didn't know how."

"Sure. You'll be all plugged in when you try it the next time, right?"

He sat by her at dinner, allowing her to cut his meat, content to share her with the others at the table while he gave his attention to the food on his plate.

Later, he insisted on a pre-bedtime session in his sister's room after his bath. Round and angelic looking in white pajamas and red fuzzy slippers, he raced back and forth until La Dawn scooped him up and carried him, loudly protesting, to bed.

She returned to close the door and shake her head, laughing. "You guys don't know what you're missing. Little brothers are a whole other thing, let me tell you."

"If you ever get tired of that one, send him down to me," Susie said lazily. Stretched out on one of the beds, she propped one ankle across the other knee and studied the revolting size of her foot. She hadn't been able to wear her mother's shoes since she was twelve. Unreal, her feet.

La Dawn flopped in the chair she dragged between the beds when the three girls wanted to talk in her room. "Okay, Pamela, here's the rundown on jobs," she said, her voice brisk. "I checked with the newspaper office and the Jobs for Youth lady down at the Y, and there's a list posted on the library bulletin board."

As she listened, Pam gave herself a manicure, applying two coats of pale pink polish, carefully blowing each nail dry before proceeding to the next.

Susie, propped on one elbow, studied La Dawn. As usual, after a few moments, she had reached up for Brotherbear and perched him on her knee, occasionally stroking the mottled fur with one slim finger.

The topic of summer jobs exhausted at last, Susie asked curiously, "How come you've kept Brotherbear all these years? I mean, the only stuff I have from when I was little — well, either my father gave it to me or — it had some connection with him. So I just wondered about — "

"The Brothuh?" La Dawn held him at arm's length over her head and let him bounce into her lap. "Oh, I don't know. I suppose he's sort of symbolic. When I first got him, he was someone — something I really loved. But still I had to change him with all that grubby shoe polish so I could love him more. So he was more like me." She added, her brown eyes serious, "I reckon I can't part with Brotherbear until I figure out, you know, whether or not that was the way to go. Then I won't need him any more."

After a short silence, Pam commented softly, "It's hard giving something up, something you've had for a long, long time, even when you don't need it any more, even when you know you'd be better off without it."

Both her friends turned to stare at her. The little girl squirmed with embarrassment and gave an uncertain giggle. "Well — you know what I mean, don't you?"

"Yeah, we know." Susie rolled onto her back once more. "We'll be scared a lot more next year about this time. Graduation. Jobs. College." She went on fiercely, "I really hate it when everything changes."

"You shouldn't do that." La Dawn propped her bare feet on the edge of the chair, hugging her knees beneath her chin. "It's kind of a torn feeling, I admit. One part of me gets excited about what's coming up next, and the other part hangs back where it's safe and happy and secure. The place inside where you're torn — that's where it hurts — "

They were quiet for a moment, thinking about that, accepting the way La Dawn had described the thing they were all feeling, a bitter-sweet ache because something known was ending, something unknown about to begin.

CHAPTER
SEVEN

By the end of June the weather had turned warm and consistently sunny, the sky a dazzling shade of blue that Susie loved. She remembered when she was little she used to lie in the grass in the back yard, dreaming about being a princess in a long beautiful dress of that exact color.

The sky would be a paler milkier blue during July and August when the humidity soared along with the mercury. In weather like that, clothing clung to damp sticky bodies. And hair like Susie's, that curled slightly during the rest of the year, turned frizzy and unmanageable during the dog days.

In the weeks after school closed, she hurried from one end of Parkdale to the other, keeping her fingers crossed that she would find a job in some nice air-conditioned office. After the first few days, however, she realized she would be lucky to find any kind of job at all. There was fierce competition for every position open, a line waiting everywhere she went, not only of high school kids but of college kids, as well, home for the summer and just as eager for those weekly paychecks.

Nora mentioned at breakfast one morning that Casey had seen a help-wanted sign in the window of the Pick o' Chicken place a few blocks over on Central Street.

Casey nodded. "Quite a turnover in the place. New girl at the cash register every time I go in."

Glancing at him, Susie wondered if he were using reverse psychology, putting the place down so she would be sure to apply for the job. But why should he care one way or the other?

He smiled at her. "Wouldn't hurt to give it a try," he said. "Maybe a lot of people just can't stand being around southern fried chicken."

Susie made a face. "DeHaven used to work in one of those places. Now he turns green if he even sees a piece of chicken. Oh well, he's such an oinker when it comes to food, especially if it's free, he probably just stuffed his face once too often. I'll go see about the job. When do they open?"

"Ten, I think," Nora said. "Why don't you wander over there a few minutes beforehand? Then you'll be first in line."

Susie thought that might be a good idea. Accordingly, at ten o'clock, she was sitting on a stone bench across the street in time to see the 'Closed' sign flipped to 'Open' by an unseen hand inside the place.

It was a fairly new building, square, built of block painted a light green, with white trim around the windows and door. A sign on the roof showed the silhouette of a chicken in the foreground, behind it a grinning farmer in green overalls. Beneath was the legend in green letters: Get the best of the bird at Pick o' Chicken.

As she pushed open the glass door, a soft bell chimed above it. But no one appeared from the back, although she could hear muffled voices and a clatter of pans. Susie stood looking at the green and white posters on the walls, urging extra purchases of cole slaw or macaroni salads, hot dinner rolls, and pies 'like mother *wishes* she could make.'

She hunched her shoulders, nose twitching slightly at the smell of cooked chicken mixed with a vagrant wisp of pine disinfectant from the recently mopped floor.

The glass counters on either side of the cash register were none too clean, she noted, observing the outer room with unaccustomed interest. Nor had the floor been mopped very thoroughly. There was a buildup of dirt around the edges and in the corners.

"Help you?"

Susie jumped and looked around to see a

thin blonde girl staring at her with small, almost colorless eyes. Her green-and-white cap and striped pinafore were spotted and wrinkled, her manner so hostile Susie could almost feel the vibrations from the other side of the counter.

"I wondered about the 'help wanted' sign," she began, a little put off by the girl's sullen expression.

"So what did you wonder?"

Susie's mouth opened, snapped shut. At last she said evenly, as deliberately as she might have spoken to a child, "I wondered if the job was still open."

The girl shrugged. "Far's I know. Manager's got his office in the rear. If all's you see is a run-down shack, that's it."

She looked Susie over, a slow, insulting inspection. Again she shrugged, the gesture implying a complete disinterest in the problem, and went back through the door to the kitchen leaving Susie with her cheeks burning.

It would be a kick working with the Duchess, she thought wryly. A real sweetheart, that one. Tempted to check the job off her list, she hesitated outside for a moment, then slowly made her way to the back of the lot. If this had been the first place she applied for work, she would have skipped it, but now it looked as if it might be her last chance for a summer job.

Behind the brightly painted building stood a small, gray, tumbledown structure, shutters hanging awry from the windows, ragged holes in the rusty screen door. Well, the Duchess had been right about one thing, Susie thought. She called it a run-down shack, and that's exactly what it was.

Approaching the door, she could see the dim interior clearly enough to be even more unfavorably impressed. An old littered desk, a day bed covered with a ratty faded quilt, a couple of straight chairs. There were file cabinets against one wall and shelves containing a few books, file folders, and messy stacks of paper.

A tall man with a hayseed haircut in a smooth circle low on his neck stood thumbing through a stack of papers on one corner of the desk. He squinted through the smoke drifting from the stub of a cigarette in his mouth.

Glancing up, he saw Susie standing at the door. "Come in! Come right on in, Lovie!"

Susie obeyed, perching uneasily on the straightback chair he indicated. "I saw your sign," she said, "and the girl at the counter said to — she said to come back and see you. About the job, I mean."

A couple of flies buzzed in a corner of the window behind him as the man looked her over. Several uncomfortable seconds ticked by.

His eyes were narrow and black, curiously flat as he fixed an unblinking stare on her. A sudden small smile of approval lifted his thin-lipped mouth on one side, but the warmth did not reach those narrow eyes.

"My name's Sooner. Buck Sooner," he said abruptly. "And you're — ?"

"Susie Kettering."

"Ah. Well, Susie, how do you feel about selling chicken?"

With an effort, she kept all expression from her face, hoping her eyes wouldn't hint at the contempt she felt for the seedy looking man watching her. It must be her lucky day, for sure, she thought. First the once-over and curt dismissal from the boney blonde inside, now the cute questions from this good ole boy.

Buck Sooner. It sounded like a good handle for a broken-down cowboy actor. Or maybe a fugitive from Nashville, the kind they ran out of town for shady dealings with the folks from the Grand Old Opry.

She sighed. "I really don't feel much one way or the other about selling chicken, Mr. Sooner," she said. The hell with putting on a phony act. She sure wasn't about to beg for a crummy job like this one.

He must have seen a hint on her face of what she was thinking. He laughed, an odd high-pitched sound, another contradiction in a man who spoke in a harsh growl.

"At that, you might add a little class to my establishment." He paused significantly before the last word, then winked at her, sharing the joke.

Susie felt a cold dislike growing with every word he spoke. Buck was obviously one of those men convinced that young girls found them attractive. Why was it that the really gross ones thought they were a natural for every woman from eight to eighty?

"Okay, Lovie," he said easily. "We only pay minimum, but you get in the hours. Ten to eight, time off for lunch and dinner. You gotta make out this form for now. Then you can go let Kit break you in. Not much to learn except the cash register and how to close up at night. Smart girl like you won't have a bit of trouble."

"Uh — thanks," Susie said. She settled at a corner of the desk which he cleared for her, and hastily printed the required information on the form. Outside, she took a deep breath, trying to clear her lungs of stale smoke and the musty damp smell in the office shack.

In the outer room of the green block building, Kit greeted her without enthusiasm. "Hired you, huh? Figured."

Susie followed her back to the kitchen area where a balding fat man and a young black were busy loading pieces of chicken into the big pressure cookers.

"Mac and Coley," Kit said, gesturing with her thumb. Her nails were bitten so that the tips of her fingers bulged over them. "Buck's just hired — what'd you say your name was? — for the front."

Susie supplied her name and said, "Hi, Coley" to the boy who had once sat across the aisle from her in geometry.

The fat man grunted, and Coley grinned and said, "Hey, Susie."

"They cook," Kit said unnecessarily. "First the stuff goes in the pressure cookers and then it's dipped in batter and then it goes on racks in the ovens. When it's done, he packs to order."

Another jerk of her thumb.

Susie hadn't seen the other boy sitting on the floor with his back against a cupboard door. He had dark brown hair with a million freckles, and as she turned to him, he gave her a wide friendly grin.

"If she's telling you we're one big happy family, don't believe a word of it," he said dryly.

Kit threw a Pick o' Chicken box at him. "That'd be the day," she said in a nasty tone. Then, to Susie, "Come on, I'll get your cap and apron. You'll have a shelf back here for your stuff, but you better keep your wallet on you."

She opened a cupboard in the hall that ran the length of the building, dug out a green-and-white cap and pinafore, and tossed them to Susie.

"This here's your shelf," she said, "and don't forget I warned you about watching your money. You get ripped off, it's your problem. The door down at the end, that's the john. I better get you squared away on the cash register. They start coming in pretty soon now."

She was right. Susie caught on to the register quickly, and she soon discovered the dark-haired boy worked rapidly and efficiently when the orders began to stack up on his spindle.

It was Kit who hung back, re-arranging the pies in the display cases, wiping the glass with a grimy rag, while Susie waited on the customers. When the lunch hour was over and Susie took a deep breath and looked around, the blonde girl had disappeared.

A head appeared over the packing work-table behind her. "She does that," the packing boy confided. "The vanishing act, right when we're the busiest. She's got it down to a fine art."

"I figured she was just off on her lunch break."

"Oh, she is, she is. She'll take an extra half hour today now she's got you stuck at the register." He waved a ham sandwich in one freckled paw. "Susie, I bet you didn't bring your lunch, did you? Not knowing whether you'd be lucky enough to get hired — "

He made a face, then laughed and continued cheerfully, "although the luck may be all on our side. Come on back here. I'll give you some of this. I've got a mother who cooks like there's no tomorrow, so we gotta eat it all today."

Susie said gratefully, "I am a little hungry. Thanks a lot. I don't think Kit ever did say what your name was?"

"Call me N.C. And if you don't ask me what that stands for, you can call me any time." On a counter at one side of the door he tossed her a sandwich in a waxed bag, put a package of cookies between them, and reached for the door of a small refrigerator. "We got Cokes and beer and Seven-Up and — "

"Oh, a beer would be great! My tongue's hanging out." Susie peered back into the kitchen. "Doesn't it get horribly hot in summer?"

N.C. handed her the beer. "It goes from hot to horrible to frying temperature — for humans, that is. The only time we get the fan is when old Buck is on hand himself to help out the peasants."

Susie finished the beer in a hurry. N.C. raised his eyebrows and laughed, but he got her another. "The only one you have to watch around here is your playmate in front," he said. "Even Buck is pretty loose — about everything but salaries."

He chewed the corner of his lip for a moment as he eyed her thoughtfully. "You and Kit, you could have heavier problems with him than the rest of us. But Kit can take care of herself, and now that you've met him, you've got the picture."

Susie nodded and smiled. It was cute of N.C. to warn her about Buck, she thought, and obliquely about Kit — and certainly nice of him to share his lunch, as well.

It would be a long day, she thought then. Maybe she could sneak another beer in an hour or two. Tomorrow, she'd bring her thermos.

CHAPTER EIGHT

By the first week in July the heat in the Pick o' Chicken building during the afternoon was almost unbearable. Mac and Coley brought in their own fan for the kitchen area, but Kit's continual nagging about a fan for the outer room only made Buck surly.

She said to him one afternoon, angrily, "Well, if you don't care about us, how about the customers? You stay back of this counter a while, you'll get an earful. And all that griping's for waiting only five minutes or so for their orders. We're in this hotbox all day."

Buck looked at her, his black eyes cold. Then he turned to Susie, who was watching them indifferently. "How you feel about it, Lovie? Want I should get you a fan in here?"

"Well — sure."

He nodded and winked at her, a chummy just-between-us expression, one eye pulled down toward the upturned corner of his thin mouth.

"Okay," he said agreeably, as if the subject had never come up before. "Let's get us another fan."

When he left, Kit stared at Susie for a long moment. "You got somethin' goin' with ole Buck?"

Susie made a soft sound of disgust. "Thanks a lot. You're sure impressed with my taste, aren't you? And whatever gave you an idea like that, anyway? He calls you Lovie, too, doesn't he? Of all the urpy people I know, old Buck has got to be at the head of the list. Number One."

"Yeah?" Kit tilted her head back, small hostile eyes looking down her thin nose in the way she had when she wanted to send somebody a message.

She had made Susie uncomfortable the first few days on the job. That is, unless she happened to be suffering even more discomfort because she wanted a drink and couldn't sneak out to get one from her thermos. Now, abruptly, she had had it with Kit and her sour disposition. Tipping her own head back, she stared at the other girl, deliberately mocking her gesture.

The blonde girl flushed. "I shoulda known. First, you get real friendly with that lousy fink,

N.C. And now you're playin' games with the boss." She snorted. "Lots of luck. Hope you got the stomach for it."

With difficulty, Susie kept her face blank, unconcerned. At the mention of her stomach, she felt it squirm uneasily, reminding her of a more vital problem than this bickering session with Kit. She would wait an hour before she went back for a quick one, she thought. But it was only a little more than half an hour before she made an excuse and left Kit to cover the front.

She made a point of standing behind the cupboard door. Buck had come along the hall a few days ago and glanced at the thermos with a knowing smile, though he said nothing. Now she hastily swallowed half a cup of juice and vodka, then sipped the rest.

She frequently played the waiting game these days. If she could slip in a beer now and then, she could go three hours between drinks. Usually, she tried to wait at least two hours, wagering with herself, but more and more often she lost the bet.

"Who you hiding from?"

N.C.'s voice behind her made her jump so she almost dropped the cup. "Don't do that!" she said irritably. "I get dehydrated up front. Once the sun starts coming in, it's horrible."

She looked at him then with new interest, recalling Kit's harsh words. It wasn't the first time she had called N.C. a fink, her tone hinting at certain secret knowledge.

"How come Kit's so down on you?" Her voice was casual. "She never misses a chance to cut you."

N.C. lounged against the opposite wall by the open window, although the air from outside was several degrees warmer than that in the hall. He gave her a wide grin, his teeth startlingly white in his flushed freckled face.

"Some people just don't appreciate my sense of humor," he said, "or they think I'm trying to be funny when I'm dead serious. Ever notice how certain people get uptight when you're honest with them?"

"So what did you say to her, being so dead serious and honest and all?"

N.C. shrugged. "She asked me to a party, and I told her I didn't think she'd like me. I'm not her type."

"Is that all?"

He nodded.

After a moment, Susie began to laugh. It was so typical of this crazy redhead, reversing the point he wanted to make, but kindly, tactfully. He didn't like Kit. On her very best day, she would never be his type.

Buck obviously disliked her, too, and the guys in the kitchen made no secret of the way they felt about her. There were times when Susie almost felt sorry for Kit. Then the thin blonde girl would make a really rotten remark or disappear during the rush hour, leaving

73

Susie to cope with a long line of customers. And the vague feeling of compassion would evaporate in a hurry as she told herself she had been right about Kit in the first place.

"On the other hand," N.C. said, his eyes amused, "I might be your type. Care to find out, say tomorrow night? Payday? That science fiction flick at the Vogue? Air conditioned. Am I playing your music?"

Susie sighed. "Right on key. Sounds great." She grinned at him. "We're both on Kit's list, you know that?" She explained what had happened an hour before. "There's old Buck standing behind the counter where it's ten degrees hotter than a sauna, asking me, do we need a fan? Unreal. When I said, sure, and he said, okay, Kit promptly added two and two about Buck and me and got — well, you know what she got." Again, she felt a twinge of anger.

N.C. chuckled. "You're not her type, either. Let's not ask her to the movies, okay?" He lifted a hand in a lazy salute and strolled back to the kitchen door.

When Susie returned to the counter, Kit looked at the clock and muttered, "Now it's my turn." Then she disappeared through the hall door, and Susie knew she wouldn't see her again until the late afternoon rush.

The streaks on the glass display cases had been bothering her lately, so she set to work polishing them. The drink had given her a temporary lift of energy, but it was dissipating when the outer door opened and La Dawn came in.

"Hey, slave, it's my early afternoon. Thought I'd come over and shake things up a little." She fanned herself with her newspaper. "Talk about raising the devil, he'd feel right at home around here. When you said it gets hot, you weren't just kidding."

"We're getting a *fan*." Susie nodded toward the corridor where Kit had headed. "Tell you about it some other time."

La Dawn caught on. She had heard about Kit. "Going to the park party tomorrow night?"

"Oh, no! Is there a party?" Susie wailed. "I just told N.C. I'd go see the movie at the Vogue. Well, maybe — "

"Don't you dare back out on N.C.!" La Dawn protested. She had heard a great deal about him, too. In fact, Susie suspected she had pumped Coley, a friend of Tony's, about his redheaded co-worker. These days, La Dawn seemed to know more about N.C. than Susie did.

Baiting her, Susie said, "I can see the movie any time."

"You can go to a park party any time, too," La Dawn said firmly, swallowing hook and all. "Listen to me, Susie, this N.C.'s a very classy dude — for a honky type, naturally. So why blow the whole thing before you even go out with him the first time? You can always make the party after the movie, can't you?"

Susie stared at her. "How come you're making such a big deal out of a little old dumb date for the moving pictures?" she drawled.

La Dawn might have blushed. It was practically impossible to tell about a thing like that. Susie had asked her once if black people blushed. The other girl gave it serious thought before she said, well, sure. Probably they did. Anyway, her cheeks felt hot when she was embarrassed about something.

"I just like the idea of you being with somebody nice. Like N.C." she said now, softly.

"And not at the party with evil people who give me hard liquor, isn't that more like it?" Susie smiled. There had been amusement in her voice, too, but she knew La Dawn realized that the question was serious, that it called for an honest answer.

"I think N.C. might be a very good friend to you, Susie," she said at last. "He wouldn't hurt you — or let you get hurt — when he was around. So what can I tell you? I'm a friend of yours, myself. I just like the idea of people lookin' out for you, bozo. Sometimes, you don't seem to care if you get hurt or not."

The bell over the door jingled as two ladies came in, their plump faces pink and moist.

"Anyway, think about it," La Dawn said and waved as she went out.

Susie did, with the same mixture of emotions she might have felt about Nora fussing over her. They did care about her, both of them. She knew that. So why couldn't they understand her as much as they loved her? Why couldn't one person know somebody else hurt inside without having to be told, having it all spelled out?

There had been a girl in her gym class last year, a Diane something, a mousy little girl. Nobody paid much attention to her. And then one Monday morning the story went all over school about how she tried to commit suicide.

They never saw her again. Her parents shipped her away to relatives in California, one of the girls in the gym class said. They were probably ashamed of what she tried to do, Susie thought, when they should have been worrying about themselves for not picking up on their own daughter's despair.

Why was it so hard for people to do that? Susie thought now, wearily. She could understand why La Dawn might be confused about problems that were different from any she'd had in her own life. But why couldn't Nora guess, at least, that something was wrong?

Nobody sensed how miserable she felt, how unhappy she was. No one could feel what she felt, that cold vacuum inside, or know what it was like to be so frightened, her insides shaking so badly, it seemed that anybody should see it. There was only one thing that made the shaking stop, that made the fear go away, that warmed the cold, cold hollowness inside —

Kit left early, mumbling something about a

dentist's appointment, her pale eyes daring Susie to argue about it.

By that hour, Susie was so hot and tired she knew she had better keep her mouth shut. It was either that or spout off and maybe get herself fired. Closing the register, she thought crossly, it would be a pleasure to tell that mean blonde where she could get off. Maybe on her last day here she would indulge. That would be something neat to look forward to.

Buck stuck his head around the hall door and grinned as he held up a tall iced drink. "How about one for the road?"

Susie brushed her hair back from her hot sticky face.

"Man, that sure looks good."

"Come on back and see what a special drink I can mix. I just came in for more ice."

Susie hesitated, torn between her dislike for the man and the thirst that had tormented her all day. Well, probably some of the guys would go back for a drink, too, she decided. Even if they didn't, she could handle Buck. And she could sure use a drink. Her thermos had been empty for hours.

Back in the shack, she found Buck alone, feet propped on the desk, country music coming from a transistor in the corner. There was a cool breeze from the fan humming on the windowsill.

Susie accepted a drink gratefully, a long strong one, vodka with only a splash of

Seven-Up. She held herself down to two, and Buck didn't push her. In fact, he never moved from his chair except when he was mixing the drinks.

She had been right about him, Susie thought, feeling a slight buzz now. It was just a nice, warm, comfortable edge that dulled the bad parts of today, the heat and the crabby customers and the unpleasant scene with Kit.

"If ever you want to buy a bottle," Buck said, nodding at the open liquor cabinet, "just say the word. I know you kids get hassled some when you want to buy a little booze, and there's no sense to it. Just remember, old Buck's always got a spare jug."

Susie got to her feet. "Thanks. That's nice of you, Buck. Maybe tomorrow night when I get paid, okay?"

"Sure, sure." He smiled up at her. "I like to keep all my people happy. We're all on the same team, sweetheart. Any time I can do favors for my people, any time at all, all you got to do is say the word."

CHAPTER
NINE

It had been one of the better park parties, Susie thought ruefully, and they had missed most of it. The movie, a double feature, showed the science fiction one last on the bill. By the time they got to the park, it was almost eleven.

La Dawn and Tony were just leaving as they arrived, but they stayed around for a few minutes to get acquainted with N.C.

La Dawn didn't try to hide her interest. "Hey, man," she said at last on a note of awe, "you'd look gorgeous in technicolor, you know that?"

N.C.'s face and right shoulder managed to shrug at the same time, denying any credit. "You people are the bottom line," he said humbly, "when it comes to living color."

Tony grinned. "She had that coming," he

said, then glanced at the lively scene behind them. "The cops have been by a couple times already," he said. "You might keep it in mind. If those turkeys can't keep the noise down, they're going to get rousted out of this little outdoor playground."

He was right about that. Shortly after midnight, a patrol car appeared, and two, large, humorless cops announced that the party was over.

Susie groaned. She'd had a couple of drinks — well, maybe three — and was discovering to her delight that N.C. danced very well, indeed.

He seemed to fit in with the crowd, too, though it bothered her a little that he wouldn't drink anything but beer. He was a lot of fun even so, but she never felt entirely comfortable at a party with people who wouldn't get with it — like La Dawn and Tony — and go with the fun and laughter and excitement generated by one or two drinks.

After a while she began to feel as if *she* were overdoing it. She had become supersensitive about it after Mark Foster started the business of reproachful looks and needling comments every time she took her glass for a refill. Not that N.C. acted like Mark, but she wished he'd loosen up a little. He could sure have a lot more fun if he didn't limit himself to the sissy stuff.

She hoped that somebody would suggest continuing the party elsewhere, but nobody did. And N.C. seemed to take it for granted that her folks would expect her home, so that's where he took her.

"You're quite a girl, Susie," he said, serious for once, and kissed her good night so nicely she felt even more regret that the evening was over so soon.

Up in her bathroom, she sat on the floor for a while, sipping from her supply bottle, her transistor playing very softly on the counter. Finally, the warm glow ebbed to a tired feeling, so she felt she could sleep.

The next morning, she woke up crying. She couldn't even remember a sad dream, but the lost, lonely feeling persisted. She couldn't seem to stop crying. All during her shower, the tears slipped down her cheeks, mingling with the warm spray. She went back to bed for a while, her wet hair wrapped in a towel, too tired and headachy and miserable to face the day or one of Nora's hearty Saturday morning breakfasts.

The weekend inched by, hot and boring and endlessly dull. Pam was gone with Scott every time she called, and she knew La Dawn was involved with a big family reunion celebrating her parents' anniversary.

Nobody called her except Tim and DeHaven, still trying to date her although she had told them straight out she wasn't interested. After the stories she knew Greg had told them, she'd be in for nothing but more trouble. And who needed that?

It was just rotten luck that this Saturday was Kit's turn on duty. N.C. worked weekends, too, taking Mondays and Tuesdays off. He called her Saturday night, and that helped a little. But it was the thought of the bottle she had bought from Buck on Friday that gave her the biggest boost during most of those two horrible days.

For Sunday dinner Nora had ham and potato salad, everything cold so she wouldn't have to heat up the big kitchen cooking. Susie took very small helpings, but even then she felt her stomach rebelling at every bite.

Finally Nora noticed that she wasn't eating. "What's the matter, honey? Don't you feel well? I thought this morning that you looked pale, and you certainly haven't had much pep lately."

Susie blew her hair off her forehead. "It's too hot to eat," she said listlessly. "It's too hot for anything." As long as the point had been made, there didn't seem to be any sense in prolonging her misery. Pushing her plate back, she asked to be excused.

Nora nodded, frowning a little. "Are you still taking those vitamins, Susie? You should. Lots of girls your age have an iron deficiency, and they don't even realize what's wrong, why they never have any energy."

She looked over at Casey's empty cup. "More coffee, honey? Though how you can drink hot coffee in this weather is beyond me."

Susie escaped, but not before her eyes met Casey's level gaze. Casey knew all too well that vitamins weren't the answer to her lack of appetite and energy.

She held her breath for a moment before she looked away. *Go on, tell her*, she thought. If he did, it wouldn't do any good. He probably knew that by now.

As she started upstairs the front doorbell rang, and she went back to answer it. The woman standing there, still in her uniform, was a nurse who worked at the hospital with Nora. A thin graying woman, she looked a lot older than she actually was, a year or two older than Nora, perhaps.

"Hi, Mrs. Shaw. Come on in."

"Hi, Susie. Did your mother tell you about the pantsuit?"

When Susie looked blank, Julia Shaw smiled and held out a garment in a plastic cleaner's bag she had slung over one shoulder. "It's my daughter's, a Pendleton. The little idiot's put on fifteen pounds, and she can't get into it any more. She keeps saying she'll lose weight, but she won't. And now she needs the money. I told Nora if it fits you, you can have it for fifty dollars. I don't think Linda's worn it a half dozen times."

Susie slipped off the plastic bag and caught her breath. She adored blue and green plaid and the suit looked brand new and expensive.

Nora came into the hall, laughing. "I've got

a mind like a sieve, Julia. I never thought about that pantsuit again. You're a doll to bring it by." She glanced at it. "Oh, my, it's beautiful! Go try it on, honey. Maybe it's a good thing you're skinny, after all. For a Pendleton, that's a real bargain."

Upstairs, Susie got into it and checked herself in the long mirror. It looked absolutely great on her. She felt so good in it her spirits lifted in a sudden surge of happiness, and she smiled at her image in the glass. It would take practically every cent she had to buy this lovely suit, but she knew she had to have it. She desperately needed something to raise her morale, to make it possible for her to like herself for a change.

Counting the money from the little Chinese box on her dresser, she sighed and stood chewing a corner of her lip. Only loose change left. She had bought a bottle yesterday, and there was still some left in her supply bottle in the bathroom cabinet. But that wouldn't last her two weeks —

She stood for a moment in an agony of indecision. She simply had to have this pantsuit. If necessary, she could borrow the money for another bottle. Or she could cut down on the stuff during the day. Of course, she could. Anyway, she'd work something out.

Fifteen minutes after Mrs. Shaw departed, Susie was still wearing the wool pantsuit, reluctant to take it off, as if she feared she would peel off her tattered self-esteem with it. At last, however, she got back in her shorts and hung the Pendleton in the closet with the rest of her winter things.

Now she couldn't wait for the weather to get cold so she could wear it. Smiling, she pictured La Dawn's expression when she saw it. La Dawn was into fashion more than Pam. It always seemed to Susie that girls like Pam with closets full of clothes just didn't care a lot about what they wore or how they looked. Someone like La Dawn had to plan and budget her wardrobe with great care. And twice she'd been on the best-dressed list in the school paper.

La Dawn would be just as excited as she was about the pantsuit, Susie thought. If only she could call her. Well, there wouldn't be any harm in walking by her house to see if the big reunion was breaking up. She could take a small bottle in her tote bag and go on down to the park if the crowd was still in the Holland's yard.

In the bathroom, transferring the contents of the supply bottle, she remembered abruptly that her money was gone and she had decided to cut down on her drinking. Inside, she could already feel the need for the innocent-looking liquid she was pouring into a small syrup bottle. For a moment she stared at it, rubbing one sweaty hand down her thigh. This thing with the booze could get out of control, she thought uneasily.

The next moment she amended the thought, telling herself crossly she was too young to have to worry about that. For heaven's sake, couldn't she celebrate a little? After one of the draggiest weekends on record, what was the harm in a couple of drinks to her great good luck, her fantastic bargain? Tomorrow, when she was busy back at Pick o' Chicken, she would probably never even think about stopping for a drink. If she did, she'd just have to stick to Cokes, that's all.

Ten minutes later she headed out the door. The cars were still parked in front of La Dawn's house, so she strolled on by. In the park, she sat down in her own special spot between the bulging roots of an ancient tree. She had been coming here as long as she could remember, sometimes to play with dolls, sometimes with books from the library, later on sometimes with a boy.

A voice inside her mind said coolly, cruelly, *and now you're coming with your bottle*. Susie shook off the thought and drowned any remaining debate in a long fiery gulp of vodka. Fifteen minutes later, the vodka was gone, but she did feel a whole lot better.

She lay on her back watching a spectacular sunset in the western sky. People said that smog had something to do with really pretty sunsets, she recalled, and felt an ache of sorrow for one more thing gone wrong with the world.

"Susie, you all right?"

Dazed, she blinked up at La Dawn standing over her, tight-faced, her eyes big and alarmed.

"Sure — sure — of course, I'm all right," she said, sitting up slowly in case she wasn't. Funny how she had nodded off like that. Must have overdone it, finishing off that bottle too fast.

"What time is it?"

La Dawn stared at her for a moment before she answered. "Almost seven. The little kids have been here playing on the swings. I just came down to get them and — I saw you."

For the first time Susie noticed Monrovia Taylor behind his sister, peeking out at her. His face, too, was serious, closed, except for his big scared eyes.

"What's the matter, Monrovia Taylor?" she said lightly. Horrified, she heard a phony note in her voice that she had never heard before. Next thing she would be saying to him coyly, cutely, "Whatsamatter, little boy? Cat got your tongue?"

When he didn't reply, she leaned toward him and said with sudden sharpness, "I said, what's the matter? What're you staring at?"

One small hand reached for his sister's. He swallowed. His voice sounded oddly strained. "You just look funny, that's all."

"Didn't you ever see anybody sleeping before?" she asked again in the harsh voice she couldn't seem to control.

"Susie, please — "

But Monrovia Taylor's voice cut across his sister's. "You look funny," he said loudly. "Your eyes look *funny*. And it's not my fault!" He let go of La Dawn's hand and raced away.

After a long moment, La Dawn said with tears in her voice, "Susie, I'm sorry."

"Well, don't be." Susie got to her feet, steadied herself against the tree, and took a deep breath past the raw hurt in her throat, the pain deeper down that felt as if something were cutting her inside.

"What you mean is, you're sorry for me," she said with all the dignity she could summon. "And if you are, I wish you'd do me a big favor. Kindly keep it to yourself."

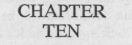

CHAPTER
TEN

Susie dragged herself out of bed that Friday, not at all sure she would make it to work. It had been the longest, most miserable week of her life.

For one thing, she had neither seen nor heard from La Dawn. She told herself firmly that she was not about to go crawling and apologizing for a dumb thing like that scene at the park. She hadn't done anything to apologize *for*.

Hadn't she always accepted La Dawn for what she was, good and bad? And nobody, not even La Dawn, was perfect. If a friend couldn't manage to accept her the same way, well, she wasn't a true friend. It was time she found out, Susie thought, before it hurt more than it did right now.

It would have helped to talk to somebody about it, even little Pam. She would never take sides in an argument, but she was undeniably as good a listener as she was a chatterbox. But she and her parents always went up to the Wisconsin Dells for the month of July. They had been late leaving this year. It meant they might not be back until the first part of August.

That week, nobody that Susie knew came in the Pick o' Chicken place except for a couple of the flakiest kids in the park crowd, Tim and DeHaven. All they could talk about were the stories going around about Greg Livingston, of how he'd totaled his father's car and spent the night in the drunk tank.

"Seems there was some chick with him," DeHaven told her with a knowing grin. "She got away. I don't suppose you'd have any idea who she was?"

Susie stared at him coldly. "If I did, I wouldn't share the news with you, old buddy."

She felt a mild curiosity herself about the girl who had been with Greg. Whoever it was, she wouldn't be talking about the escapade.

Well, there was one thing for sure. When DeHaven went out the door, he would be sharing his version of the truth all over town.

Nobody would get a straight story from Greg, either, because he had disappeared. Most people suspected his parents had sent him away until things cooled down. Greg had done quite a bit of damage to someone's property; a fence, a couple of trees, and a garage door. Rumor had it the property owner was threatening a lawsuit. Doubtless that had a bearing on Greg's disappearing act.

It was hot and humid all that week, a smothering, heavy, moist heat that made it hard to breathe. The weather brought on the itching irritation of prickly heat, and after the third or fourth day, it affected the most even and amiable of dispositions.

Susie went to work every day with her stomach churning with nausea even before she smelled the chicken cooking back in the kitchen. Friday morning she stood under the cold shower for several minutes, hoping the shock would get her going.

She seemed to be plodding along day after day, not daring to look ahead for more than a few hours. Despite her good resolutions and all the promises to herself, her bottle was almost empty. And this was her weekend on duty.

At that point she forced her thoughts to retreat, detouring them to something else. Otherwise, the panic she felt soared to crisis proportions. At times like that she couldn't trust herself not to do something really stupid.

She stepped out of the shower, her skin a mottled bluish color, but the air warmed her quickly. Too quickly. The temperature hadn't been below 95° day or night for what seemed an eternity, actually about ten days.

Dressing quickly, she went down to the

kitchen hoping there would be coffee left on the stove. Sometimes that helped give her a much-needed lift in the morning, and today she lacked enough energy to make a new pot.

There was enough left to fill one of the small persimmon-colored mugs she had given Nora for Mother's Day. She stood leaning against the counter sipping tentatively in case her stomach gave a lurch of rebellion as it sometimes did on a bad morning. Then she saw Nora's purse on the little built-in desk by the door.

Susie stiffened, the mug halfway to her lips. Nora always carried a lot of cash with her. After a bad experience with credit when she was newly widowed, she had torn up her credit cards in disgust, raging about a male dominated world bent on tormenting single women. Even now, no matter how Casey warned of the risks in carrying so much money, she went around with close to a hundred dollars in her purse.

She would never miss ten dollars —

Susie took two steps toward the desk, then stopped, her eyes closed tight in a sudden wave of revulsion. When had she turned into the kind of person who would steal from her own mother?

On the back porch, Nora called to the next-door neighbor. A moment later, she hurried into the kitchen on her noiseless rubber-soled shoes.

"Hi, sweetie! I'm going to be late on duty, I

guess. Can't be helped. Mrs. Hayward's mother fell again. If we'd get a decent ambulance service in this town — "

Susie raised her mug with both hands and took a swallow of coffee. "Is she all right?" she asked, her voice a bit unsteady. "The old lady, I mean?"

Her mother made a face. "I know what you mean. Yes, the old lady's probably fine. She's tough as they make them. But Mrs. Hayward fell apart as usual. Hysterics, feeling faint, you name it. I couldn't leave until we'd called in somebody to help calm her down."

She picked up her purse, frowned to herself, said absently to Susie, "Eat something now. Eat a good breakfast before you leave, dear."

"Sure, Mom," Susie said with a new surge of self-loathing.

She stood where she was for several minutes, long after she heard Nora's car leave. It seemed important that she stand in the same spot without moving, breathing slowly and with great care. Otherwise, she might fall apart like Mrs. Hayward next door, only much more quietly.

What would happen the next time she found herself tempted by Nora's purse? Would she stop again? Or would she go ahead and take the money she needed so desperately? Because she needed a bottle so desperately —

Two hours later during her morning break, she finished the last of the vodka. Replacing the thermos in her cupboard, she thought dully, *well, that's it.* When she closed the door, she saw Kit down the hall looking at her.

"Your mother's here," she said.

Startled, Susie went out front to find Nora leaning against the display case, tapping on the glass impatiently with her car keys.

"Honey, I had to go out to lunch anyway, and I thought it would be just as easy to stop by as try to get through on the phone. You know how they are at the switchboard about nurses calling outside."

"Anything wrong?" Susie asked. In the split-second way a brain has of coming forth with instant analyses of absurd remarks, her own mind commented now, *what else could possibly be wrong?*

"I may not be home tonight," Nora said. "It's Mrs. Hayward's mother. This time she's not responding well. And they can't get a private duty nurse."

"So you volunteered."

"Well, tomorrow's Saturday." Nora smiled, always vaguely apologetic about being a soft touch. "I can sleep all day if I want."

She waved at N.C., who called a greeting from the back.

"Such a nice boy," she murmured and leaned forward to say with a smile, "You like him, don't you?"

Susie grinned and shrugged. "He's okay."

Her mother nodded. "Casey was right," she

said. "N.C., he's different. Steadier. He'll be good for you."

"Casey said that?" Susie laughed. "What did he do, conduct a three-minute interview last Friday? Or does he just size up people like N.C. with X-ray vision or something?"

Smiling, Nora turned toward the door. "Silly," she said. "He knew N.C. before. Some other job he had. Didn't he tell you that? Well, I'd better run. Give Casey a call around five and let him know. You won't forget?"

"No," Susie said automatically. "I won't forget."

A moment later, she roused herself to see Kit glaring at her. "I'm going to lunch," she said, obviously repeating what she had already said before. "It's my turn for the early shift."

It wasn't, but Susie didn't feel like arguing. The last thing she wanted was food in her queasy stomach. Besides, she had to sort out what Nora had just said, what it seemed to mean.

"He knew N.C. before. Some other job he had. Didn't he tell you that?"

No, he hadn't, Susie thought. More important, N.C. had not mentioned it either.

During the next two hours, busy with the usual lunch crowd, the sound of the cash register alternating with the bell over the door, her mind went over her mother's words again and again.

She took her lunch, a banana and a ham

sandwich, back to the corridor where she sat on the wide windowsill to eat, the glass cranked out to admit any stirring of the hot still air. She managed to finish the banana, but the sandwich was too dry. At last, she wrapped it up again in the baggie and sat sipping a Coke, wishing she hadn't finished her thermos that morning, wishing the Coke would magically turn into something else, wishing she didn't feel so numb and cold inside. Which was ridiculous because she felt hot and utterly miserable on the outside.

"There you are!" It was N.C.'s cheerful voice. "You don't want to eat alone, do you?"

"Yes," Susie said flatly. "I do."

"Oh?"

"From now on," she added.

A short silence.

"What did your mother tell you?"

Susie looked at him for a moment. "She told me something I should have guessed for myself. The reason you moved in so fast my first day here, a lot of things like that." She gave a brief laugh and turned away. "After all, I'm not so — I'm not the type guys move in on like that."

"How do you know what type you are?"

Susie's head jerked up. "What's that supposed to mean?"

"I mean, if guys don't respond to you faster than they do, that's their problem. I told you the other night, Susie, you're quite a girl. I meant it." There was no expression on his face

97

except for something she couldn't read in the eyes watching her intently.

"There was something a lot more important you didn't tell me the other night," she said wearily. "You never mentioned the fact that you and Casey are old friends, that he found out you worked here when he saw the sign in the window. He steered me onto this job deliberately."

He nodded. "Yeah, that's right. Would you have understood any part of it if I had told you?"

Susie threw the bottle out the window, a violent gesture keyed to her inner turmoil. "What's there to understand?" she said harshly. "You're Casey's little spy. You and me, we've done a lot of talking lately. You know how I feel about him. It's kind of funny, isn't it? Did you take all that back to him, everything I told you?"

He winced. "You're going to discover some day, Susie, who your friends really are. I just hope it won't be too late when you find out Casey's practically Number One on the list. At least he would be if you'd let him."

But Susie didn't pay any attention to his last words.

"What do you mean — too late?" she said. "Too late for what?"

He hestitated. "Too late for you — to keep from being hurt," he said in a low voice, "hurt more than you have been already. Susie, if you'd just listen — "

"No!" She hurled the word at him, altering the tone rather than the pitch of her voice. "Kit was right about one thing, N.C. She was right about you. You *are* a fink!"

He took a deep breath, then turned on his heel.

Behind him, Susie swung her feet up onto the wide sill, knees tucked to her chest, hands hugging them close to her body. She put her cheek down on them, eyes shut, wishing she could die without suffering any more torment, the wrenching tearing hunger for a drink, the terrible hurt of betrayal. She had begun to like N.C. She liked him a lot. Now, burned in her mind was a picture of herself that was worse in many ways than any other pain.

The afternoon dragged by. She remembered to call Casey and relay Nora's message, her voice cold, without emotion. She ate the rest of her sandwich late, around seven, and barely made it back to the restroom before she vomited.

The kitchen crew departed shortly afterward, and she heard Kit slam the door in the corridor on her way out. Susie checked to make sure it was locked, closed the register, and began to turn out the lights.

Buck came in the front door, ice clinking in the glass in his hand. "Hey," he said, his crooked smile pleased with her, "how's my best girl?"

"Tired," Susie said tonelessly.

He lifted his glass. "Got just the right sort

of tonic for that tired feelin', Sweetheart."

When had he stopped calling her Lovie like he called all the other girls? Susie wondered. When had he begun calling her — but only her — *Sweetheart*?

She sucked in her breath, feeling the perspiration trickle down her back, momentarily cool on her spine.

She spoke quickly. "I've been meaning to ask — if I could buy another bottle, Buck. Except — could you take it out of my wages next Friday? I'm a little short. But if you wouldn't mind — I could — " Her voice faltered as he stood watching her, black eyes amused.

"No money?" he said, his voice oddly hushed, but full of the same secret amusement. "Well, now, I don't know — "

Her whole body screaming with need, with the devouring hunger that only one thing could assuage, Susie grit the words between her teeth.

"Please — *please* — "

He reached out to her then, one hand on her arm gently, firmly pulling her through the door where he held her close to him.

"Oh, now, sure, little Sweetheart. You just come along back to the office. You and old Buck, we'll work somethin' out. You just come along, and we'll see about it."

CHAPTER ELEVEN

Every morning when La Dawn opened her eyes, she found it waiting for her on the edge of her thoughts, something that pounced only when she was awake. She couldn't remember a misunderstanding with Susie that had lasted longer than a few hours. Neither of them was capable of carrying a grudge.

Twice in the past, she recalled, Susie had come down to her house looking utterly miserable to protest, "Best friends aren't supposed to fight. They're supposed to get together and *talk* things over."

And at least once she had gone to Susie first to say they had better make up fast because nothing could be worth the kind of misery she was suffering. But now the days passed with anger and coldness between them, without any word from Susie.

There was a difference this time. Susie had been shamed. Clearly it had cut deep. Monrovia Taylor's blunt reaction to the way she looked in the park that day, her eyes red and puffy, a glazed look in them. Her pride had been hurt by what he said, and pride was always a delicate thing to heal.

La Dawn got out of bed and stuck her head out the hall door to see if the bathroom was empty. It was. She grabbed her clothes and hurried to take her shower before Aunt Bea came up to clean the second floor.

Her aunt stayed with them summers, now that La Dawn was working, too, to keep an eye on her little brothers and help with the cleaning and cooking. Aunt Bea's husband was pretty much of a loser, La Dawn suspected, though her aunt seemed to be crazy about him.

Valadia Holland had once tried to explain that puzzling infatuation. "Honey, when you love somebody, you see things in that person nobody else can see. Maybe those things aren't there for anybody but you. So when you hear people saying love's a kind of magic sometimes, that's generally what they mean."

Magic, La Dawn mused, even for a loser. And maybe for somebody in big trouble, too — like Susie? A lot of the kids were spreading stories about her these days. La Dawn was aware of the rumors through fragments that she had overheard in the library. Doubtless the girls had meant for her to overhear what they were saying.

Susie was really a great person. She was going through a terrible, mixed-up period, that's all, and the booze had gotten to her. La Dawn was sure about that.

Out of the shower, she reached for her towel, making a face when she felt the damp corner. No matter how much they were preached at or pounded on, her little brothers grabbed the first towel handy. Nothing was sacred in the upstairs bathroom, that was for sure.

She went back to her room to fix her face and hair. Should she eat breakfast first? Or should she go immediately to do the thing she had been agonizing about all week? Again, she felt nervous flutters in her stomach. No sense in eating until she had done what she had to do.

Looking at herself in the mirror, she saw the scared look in her eyes and made a soft sound of exasperation. For heaven's sake, Nora Sears was a rational person. Why should it be a big thing, talking to her about Susie?

The mirror reflected her dim view of an idiotic question like that one. She hadn't the vaguest idea of how Nora would react when she tried to spell out Susie's problem, one she knew very well Nora refused to recognize. It would be a rough session. There couldn't be any doubt about that.

For days La Dawn had debated with herself

about the best thing to do. Susie needed help. Fact. No question there. And she, La Dawn, couldn't get through to her no matter how hard she tried. Fact. Then, who could help her? And how? Naturally, Susie's mother seemed the best bet, if somebody could open her eyes to what was happening.

But would it do any good if Susie felt betrayed by the person who talked to her mother? She would feel that way, of course. And would it help anybody at all if Nora still refused to believe the truth, that the daughter she adored was an alcoholic?

At last, La Dawn went to her mother for advice. Late Friday night she said good night to Tony on the steps and slipped into the quiet house to find Valadia having a last cup of coffee in the kitchen as she made out her weekly shopping list.

"Got a minute, Mom?"

Her mother looked up, startled, then smiled at the familiar question, the usual lead-in to family discussions.

La Dawn sighed. "I've got a problem that has me climbing the walls. I can't figure out which way to turn."

Her mother said nothing, waiting.

"It's about one of my friends." La Dawn traced the pattern in the plastic tablecloth with her index finger. "This girl, she's heading for trouble. And she won't listen to anybody. I've tried talking to her, though I haven't said too much — she cuts me off too quickly. But I'm sure her mother can't see what's happening. I don't even know if she'd believe it if — if somebody told her."

Almost in tears, she looked up at Valadia. "The way it looks to me, that's the only chance this girl has to get help — if somebody talks to her parents."

Valadia sipped her coffee, round face thoughtful. "Is your friend — is she on drugs, La Dawn?"

La Dawn hesitated. "She's drinking. I don't know how much, I just know it's an awful lot."

Valadia made a soft sound, a sound of pain. Drinking was a problem with Aunt Bea's husband, too. The knowledge lay between them, shared but unstated.

"It's a matter of priorities, isn't it?" she said at last, carefully. "You're worried about your friend, and you're just as worried about something going wrong with the friendship between you. Isn't that right? If you go and talk to this girl's parents, they may be able to help her. And they may not. In either case, she won't find it easy to forgive you for interfering, will she?"

"She'll find it *impossible* to forgive me," La Dawn murmured. But she leaned back in her chair. Her mother had a way of going right to the heart of the problem. Even when she pointed out painful truths, it was a relief somehow to see the way out of a muddle of confusion.

"You think I'd better gamble, don't you?" she said. "If there's any chance at all that it might do some good, well, I have to try. Even if she never speaks to me again."

Her mother leaned across the table to touch her cheek with gentle fingers. "If it helps, honey, I want you to know this kind of thing happens to every one of us sooner or later. We get mixed up about things like love and loyalty. I always ask myself, am I more concerned about the friend — or the friendship? Which is more important?"

La Dawn nodded. "Well, have you ever lost a really good friend because you had to do something — because you had to choose? And you chose the best thing for the friend?"

Valadia took a deep breath. Her eyes were bright with tears, but she smiled as she nodded.

"And you could live with it afterward?"

"Yes. Yes, I could live with it. Because I could live with myself. Regret can eat away at your insides, baby. The fewer times you have to think, *if only I'd done this or that,* the happier person you'll be. But if you can look back and know you tried, no matter how things work out — yes, you'll find you can live with it."

La Dawn shook her head slowly. "It just doesn't seem right, though. I've been really worried about Su — about this girl."

Her mother didn't appear to notice her slip.

"I've been just sick about what's happening to her. So why should it work out that if I try to help her, we won't be friends any more? It looks like I'm damned if I do and damned if I don't."

"Maybe it won't work out that way, La Dawn. I'm willing to bet you'll feel better, though, if you make an honest attempt to help — even if this girl's folks won't listen. Sitting around worrying about something, that can be the hardest thing ever."

She added, her eyes troubled, "Except for the way you'd feel if something happened — and you hadn't tried."

La Dawn got to her feet. "I'll sleep on it," she said, and went around the table to kiss her mother. "Thanks, lady."

"I wouldn't be surprised if you slept better tonight." Valadia's voice was soft.

Well, she had slept better, La Dawn thought now, and checked her watch. No more stalling. They'd be through with breakfast down there, and Susie would be gone to work. If she waited any longer, Nora might be off shopping.

A few minutes later she rang the bell at the house down the street, feeling her heart hammering in her chest, a reflected beat at the back of her throat.

Casey opened the door and smiled down at her. "Hi there, La Dawn. You just missed Susie. This is her weekend to pick the chick-

107

ens — " His smile faded. "But maybe you didn't come to see her?"

La Dawn swallowed. Her voice sounded odd, but that was logical, considering the way she felt inside. "No. I — I really came to talk to Mrs. Sears. If she's not busy — "

Casey stepped back so she could come in. "Nora's asleep," he said then. "She's been on duty most of the night." As La Dawn turned to look at him uncertainly, he asked, "Will I do?"

She paused, but only for a moment. "I guess I have to talk to somebody," she said. "Oh — I didn't mean that the way it sounded."

"No offense meant, none taken." He gestured toward the kitchen. "We're serving coffee and doughnuts this morning, and I'd be happy to scramble a couple of eggs."

"Oh, no eggs, thank you. Coffee and a doughnut, that sounds great."

She ate a doughnut and drank a little coffee as Casey chatted amiably about the weather and the reason Nora had gone on special duty last night. Mrs. Hayward's mother was much better, he remarked. Her condition was stabilized now.

At last he ran out of casual conversation. He sat quietly, relaxed in his chair, one hand curled around the big mug that said Coffee For Casey on one side, waiting for La Dawn to speak.

She stirred her coffee, her gaze on the handle of the spoon. Inside she felt the nerves in her stomach relax slightly, even though she was about to burn the last of her bridges. It would be just that, too, talking to Casey when she knew how Susie felt about him. And Susie would find out sooner or later. Still, in this moment, she felt more relief than sadness.

"Susie and I, we've been friends a long time," she said. "When we moved here — that was in first grade, so I was six — she was the first girl who came up to me at recess. And we had lunch together that day and walked home and — " she gestured, palms up " — and we've been best friends ever since."

Casey made a sound of agreement.

"I remember once a long time ago," La Dawn went on, "we were talking about what we wanted to do when we grew up. And Susie said she'd like to help people, do something great all by herself. She could, you know. She could really do that."

She looked up at Casey and added fiercely, "That's why it's such a waste! Because Susie's always helping people, and she's not the kind who only does her number when somebody's there to notice, either."

"I know," Casey said.

"One time, a couple of years ago — it was during Christmas vacation — my mom got the flu. Then Monrovia Taylor came down with it right afterward. And Susie came over and spent a couple of days helping out, nursing, whatever had to be done. She said she'd had the flu and there wasn't any point in the rest of our family getting it if we could keep away from the sick ones. I just can't imagine anybody else doing something like that, especially during Christmas vacation."

"No," Casey said. "You're right about that."

"I know better than a lot of people how it is with her," La Dawn said. "She's having trouble growing up, that's all. Well, lots of kids do. She'll get there okay. She'll even make a better than average person, with a little more mileage on her. If only — "

She stopped. Again she swallowed hard. Across the room, a faucet dripped intermittently into a pan in the sink. She sensed Casey stiffen in his chair, though he made no movement that she could detect. *He knows*, she thought. *He knows what I'm going to tell him.* But the silence stretched between them.

This Casey Sears was a very nice man. La Dawn let out the breath she had been holding without realizing it. It would be all right. There really wasn't any hurry, either. He understood so well, he was going to let her say it, herself, because he knew that was the way she wanted it.

She looked straight into the intent blue eyes across from her. "Susie's got a big problem. I think you've guessed that. She's drinking too much, and she can't stop. And she won't admit she's gone way past the point where she can control it."

110

She saw a spasm of pain cross the square blunt face. Casey's mouth twisted. "Yes," he said, "I suspected as much."

La Dawn waited for a moment. Then she told him what had happened last Sunday in the park, about the estrangement since Monrovia Taylor had blurted the words that couldn't be recalled, that could never be erased.

"But now I know if I have to make a choice between Susie and me being friends again — and getting some help for her even if she hates me forever for doing it — well, the important thing is Susie."

Casey looked down, studying his thumbnail with great care, as if some vital truth were engraved upon it. "I thank you for that, La Dawn." He cleared his throat. "Susie will, too, one day."

"But what do you think would be best? Should I talk to Mrs. Sears?"

He shook his head. "No. That's why I — I sidetracked you just now. I was hoping you'd confide in me instead of Nora." He sighed heavily. "She just won't see the truth. Somehow, she just can't see it. I've been going along from day to day, probably much as you've been doing, waiting for the storm to break, waiting — "

La Dawn cut in urgently, "But can't we do something? Isn't there anything — ?"

"I don't think so. I don't think anybody can help Susie — until she wants help." He looked up, frowning, deep lines etched in his forehead and around his mouth. "I'll talk to her, La Dawn. At this point I think she should know there are people who want to help her — when she's ready. As a matter of fact — "

He pawed through his thick black hair. "As a matter of fact, there's a boy who works down at her place — N.C. they call him — he's somebody I knew, somebody I —well, anyway, I asked him to sort of keep an eye on her."

La Dawn stared at him. "N.C.?" she said in a near whisper. "Oh, wow, if Susie ever finds out you knew N.C. before— that you'd talked to him about her — "

"There's not much chance of that. No, I think that's the least of our worries."

La Dawn pushed her coffee mug aside, her stomach suddenly tied in knots. She thought unhappily, if only she could be as sure of that as he was.

CHAPTER
TWELVE

That morning during the first week of August it rained in a steady downpour for almost two hours. Lightning stitched across the sky in a dramatic display, followed seconds later by the crash of thunder.

On her morning break, Susie watched from the corridor window, remembering how electric storms had frightened her when she was little. To her, the lightning looked as if the sky were splitting open. Then, the terrible loud ripping sound of thunder seemed to verify the fact that her world was, indeed, being torn asunder.

Her father would pick her up, she recalled, to comfort her and try to explain in words she could understand that there was nothing to be afraid of. He played a little game with her in which they held their breath when the lightning flashed, then let it out in a tremendous roar, trying to drown out the sound of thunder. A few minutes later she would be laughing as hard as she had been crying before.

In the wake of the memory came a crushing wave of depression. She had no one now to help her put her world together again, to put the shine back in it. Even her father might not have been able to do that if he were alive, but he would have tried. She was sure of that, because he had cared about her.

The sad thing with people nowadays, she thought, was the way everybody went rushing around in such a hurry that most of them didn't have time to help anybody else, even if they happened to notice someone was in trouble, that someone was hurting. Nobody had time to care about anybody else.

Do I still care? she wondered, but the question submerged in the revolving pattern of her thoughts. For the most part, she decided, she kept to herself. At least she wasn't inflicting her own pain on anyone else.

Of course it was safer this way. Nobody noticed her too much. She did her thing at home and on the job as well. She talked to people when they talked to her, answering questions, always smiling, walking a tightrope on which she constantly balanced her behavior, every move, every word she spoke.

Occasionally she had the bleak, frightening feeling of being imprisoned within her skin, looking out from her eyes, but unable to convey her distress in any way.

When Mrs. Ray, the motherly librarian, came in for a chicken and cole slaw lunch, Susie would hear herself with disbelief.

"Hi Mrs. Ray, the usual? Hey, our banana cream pie's really great today. Can I tempt you?"

"Get thee behind me, Susie!" the little plump woman said in mock horror. Then she laughed, peering over her glasses into the dessert case. "Well — maybe if I took the smaller one back to share with the girls — "

"How could it hurt?" Susie agreed. Her little laugh tied it all together in a completely natural exchange of dialogue. And who could hear her crying inside, *can you see me in here?*, when the words she spoke drowned out everything else.

"Would you like the box or the basket, sir? Well, there's more chicken in the basket — "

"Yes, ma'am, the salad's extra, but you have a choice. And it's fresh and cold from the cooler — "

Smile. Smile at the little fat ladies and the tall bony ones, at the bald guys and the ones with beards or braids, at the little kids with their hot sticky pennies and nickels and dimes.

Say thank-you and come-again and have-a-nice-day. None of it means very much because you sure don't care a whole lot about whether you ever see them again or what fate waits for them. They don't even hear what you're saying, anyway, so how can they be expected to know there are tears behind the smile?

Rain sluiced down the corridor window in a steady blurring stream. Susie shivered suddenly and poured the last of the contents of her thermos in the cup. She stared at it for a moment, surprised that there was only a half inch of liquid. She could have sworn there was more than that left.

Reaching in the back of her cupboard under a sweater, she pulled out a fresh bottle. Her hands weren't shaking as much today, she noted with approval, and said to herself, *steady as you go —*

"Well, what do you know?" It was Kit's voice behind her.

Susie jumped, then finished pouring, irritated at the other girl for sneaking up on her. But she wasn't as upset as she would have been if some of the vodka had spilled. The thought amused her, and she smiled as she replaced the bottle cap.

"What's so funny?" Kit demanded. "You know what could happen to you, gettin' caught with that? I've thought for a long time you were on somethin'."

Susie closed the cupboard door, tossed off the drink in the thermos top and regarded the blonde girl calmly. "That wasn't very clever of you, Kit," she said, but without malice. Her voice was almost gentle. "I hate to tell you this, but you're practically the last to know. Just about everybody's on to my little secret by now."

Kit stared at her. "Everybody but Buck," she said at last. The tip of her tongue slid over her upper lip. "You wouldn't be here, kid, if he was onto you. Drinkin' on duty? No way is he gonna put up with that."

Susie grinned. "I can see the wheels going round and round in your head. Pretty soon they're going to go *tickety bonk*! and your eyes will light up — and then you'll make me an offer I can't refuse. Right?"

The small, almost colorless eyes narrowed. Kit snorted. "Caught you, didn't I? Got your bottle right there handy. How you gonna lie your way out of this?"

Susie thought, almost enjoying the situation, she hadn't felt so kindly toward old Kit since the first day on the job. Now, if she just swung the noose a little closer, Kit would stick her head through it all by herself.

"I'll put it right up front where you can look at it," Susie said. "I'm not going to lie."

Kit's eyes glittered. Her lips moved in a small smile. "If I said I'd keep my mouth shut — if I said nobody else has to know — how much would it be worth to you?"

Susie considered solemnly, controlling the bubble of amusement inside that threatened to erupt in a giggle and spoil everything.

"Not much," she said at last. "I keep telling

you, everybody's wise by now. So why would it matter to me whether or not you keep your mouth shut?"

It was a nice gesture, she thought, urging this girl to mind her own business before she got in trouble too. Nice? It was absolutely noble. Inside, it felt as if the brief glow from the liquor had revived, spreading through her whole body. She found the scene unreal, but very funny. She must not laugh, she told herself sternly.

Leaning toward Kit, she said, "Let it go, huh? Haven't I been doing my share of the work? You don't have anything to gripe about. So why don't you forget it?"

Kit laughed, a brittle, humorless sound. "I'm not very good at forgetting something that might be worth some extra bread. If I can't make a deal with you, I'll just try somewhere else."

She waited for a moment, watching Susie closely, as if she might be giving her a chance to reconsider. When Susie smiled and shook her head, the blonde girl flushed and walked up the hall again.

"Pity," Susie said aloud. That was the trouble with noble gestures. They were usually wasted on un-noble people.

She returned to the front at noon to relieve Kit. The new part-time girl, a tiny brunette named Ann Marie, came on for the rush hour. But when Susie came back from lunch, she found Ann Marie still on duty.

Her dark eyes held a gleam of curiosity. "I've just been hired full-time," she announced. "Buck bounced Kit out of here without even letting her stay the whole day. What did she *do*?"

Susie made a face. "She tried to cut somebody's throat," she said, "and the knife slipped."

The bell over the door jingled as a customer came in, and Ann Marie was forced to let it go. The rain had let up in time for the regular lunch crowd. The air that came through the door seemed no cooler, however, and the humidity had soared.

Susie watched the hands of the clock move with agonizing slowness to three o'clock when she took her afternoon break. The hours after the noon rush seemed endless now. For one thing, when they weren't busy, she was too conscious of N.C. standing behind the counter, quiet, seldom joking any more. Frequently she found him watching her with that same strange expression on his face.

At first, right after she told him what she thought of him, she had expected to find him waiting for her in the corridor or at the door after work. She had been sure, somehow, that he would try once more to talk to her, to rationalize the way he'd been spying on her for Casey. But he hadn't approached her again, and he spoke quite normally when anyone else was around. No one could guess they'd had a disagreement, even if someone were interested.

At three she ducked quickly out into the corridor, then stopped short. But it wasn't N.C. standing by the window waiting for her. It was Buck.

He turned and watched, unsmiling, as she walked toward him slowly, bracing herself as she saw anger smouldering in his eyes.

"I was hopin' I wouldn't have to set you straight," he said. "After all the favors I been doin' for you lately, seems to me the least you can do is behave yourself on the job."

Susie stood silently, feeling the hot blood rise to her face.

"You want to have yourself a good time after hours, coupla drinks with the boss before you go home, that's your business. That's just fine. Anythin' you do after you leave here, that's fine, too."

Both hands came out to grasp her shoulders, his long thin fingers holding them in a painful grip. He shook her once hard, then released her so quickly, she staggered back a few steps, almost falling.

"Just so it's clear between us, Sweetheart," he said softly. "If I hear you're nippin' on the job again, you're gonna be one sad, sorry little girl, understand?"

Susie leaned against the wall, her eyes closed, mouth set tight against the sob that tore at the back of her throat. And, worse, the nausea churning in her stomach.

"The bottle," he said. "Where you hidin' it?"

She swallowed bitterness, the salt of tears, a last shred of pride. "In my cupboard."

"Give it to me."

She opened the cupboard, reached for the bottle, handed it to him. But she managed to push the sweater to one side as she did so, hiding the thermos.

He looked at her for several seconds, black eyes boring into hers as if he read the thoughts behind them, the contempt, the revulsion she couldn't hide in that moment even if she had tried.

Abruptly he smiled, the lopsided smile that never seemed to warm his thin face. "Sweetheart," he said, "you're somethin' else, you know that?"

One long arm shot past her shoulder as he reached into the cupboard, threw the sweater to the floor, and brought out the thermos. Looking down at it, he shook his head and sighed.

"You're gonna have to learn," he said, but there was amusement in his voice now, as if she were a precocious five-year-old whose spirit he admired even as he pondered appropriate discipline.

"You can come get these after quittin' time," he said. "No, better still, I think I'll keep 'em in the office after this. You come back and we'll have a drink. Just to show there's no hard feelin's. Okay?"

Susie felt her eyes burn as she stared at him, unblinking, without moving.

"I didn't hear you say you were comin' to have a drink," he said after a moment. "I didn't hear you say nothin' at all."

In a momentary silence back in the kitchen, she heard somebody pop the top from a can of beer. Then Coley's voice said loudly, happily, "First one today, man! Ahhhhh, that's good!"

Turning, Susie ran up the hall to the washroom, slamming the door on the sound of Buck's laughter.

When the retching subsided at last, she sat back weakly on the dirty linoleum floor, her head sagging against the wall. A cold perspiration popped out on her forehead, little rivulets soaking into her hair.

But her tears were warm as they ran back to her ears and down to drip off her chin. There was no hope for her now. She knew that, and Buck knew it, too. Just as he knew she'd be back in his office at quitting time. For a couple of drinks — to show there were no hard feelings.

CHAPTER
THIRTEEN

She woke on Saturday to a gray world, the sky dark with the heavy clouds of a new storm coming in from the east. As she got into a tee shirt and denim shorts, she heard Casey's car leave. But when she went down to the kitchen, expecting to find her mother at the table, it was Casey who sat there, elbows propped, finishing his coffee.

He looked up at her and grinned, reading her mind as usual. "Her car has a flat," he said. "She took mine."

"That's okay with me," Susie said lightly, "if it's okay with you."

She poured some orange juice, then looked at the glass on the counter, mouth twisting as she queried her stomach. *No? Maybe some coffee first? Oh, come on, make up your mind —*

She poured a mug of coffee from the pot on the stove, then raised an eyebrow at Casey. "More?"

"Please."

She filled his cup, uneasily aware of his steady gaze. Without looking at him, she asked, "What's the matter? Is my nose on crooked?"

"Your nose is fine," he said. "You have your mother's nose, as a matter of fact, which is about as fine as a nose can get."

She had to look at him then. "You feeling all right, Casey? I mean, just because I poured your coffee for you — "

"Have I ever lied to you, Susie?"

Susie took a deep breath and let it out loudly as she turned to put the coffee pot back on the stove.

He went on in the same strange tone. "I'm serious. When you ask me — which you don't very often, I'll admit — but when you do ask me how your hair looks or if a sweater's a good color on you, have I ever told you it looks great when you know it doesn't?"

She sat down, sipping from her mug, watching him over the rim. "Casey, this is a really weird conversation, you know that?"

He gave her a wry grin. "Have we ever had a normal one? Oh, I'll give you credit for one thing. You're never rude. You never say anything out loud that you might be thinking about me. But then, you don't say much of anything at all, do you?"

Susie looked down at the spoon she was twisting between her fingers. "It's not as if we had a whole lot in common," she said warily.

"At one time I hoped — well, I hoped we

could take the one thing we do have in common, the way we both feel about your mother, and work from there."

She didn't look at him. "I'd rather not talk about it. It's too late to — "

"No, it's not too late!" He leaned toward her, his hand reaching for hers. Then, as if he thought better of it, he let it drop to the table between them in a tight fist. "Let me say what I have to say," he told her. "Then I'll go cut the lawn and leave you alone. Just listen to what I want to tell you first. Okay?"

After a moment, she nodded.

"I want to explain something to you that I don't think you understand. I know I didn't when I was your age, and I didn't have the kinds of problems you've got."

She looked up quickly at that, but he held up his hand when she would have spoken.

"We'll get to that in a minute," he said. "I'd like to convince you of one thing, Susie. There isn't anybody in this world strong enough so that he — or she — doesn't need somebody else at one time or another. Can you believe that?"

Her fingers released the spoon and it dropped onto the table, clinking against the butter dish.

"Sure," she said. "I believe that."

He looked relieved, as if he'd been prepared to argue the point. "Good," he said. "You've had me worried. I thought I'd have a hard time getting through to you."

He brought his fist down heavily on the table then, making the cups jump. "Susie, you don't have to fight this thing alone. You have people who care about you, who want to help."

She stared at him. It wasn't enough that he'd come along and taken all her mother's time and attention and caring, she thought. No, that wasn't enough for Casey. Now he wanted to take over her life, too. Just lean on big strong Mr. Wonderful and he'll fix everything.

Wait a minute. What was he hinting at? *Fight this thing alone* — Sure. And the minute she admitted anything, what would he do? He'd ship her off to one of those places for crazy drunks. Once he got her to confess she'd been drinking, he'd exaggerate about it to Nora. If he got her to admit she might possibly have a little trouble now and then — not that it was any big problem, but he'd get Nora to see it that way.

"Casey," she said, and her voice was amazingly cool and steady considering the conflict of emotion inside, "I haven't got the vaguest idea what you're talking about."

He rubbed his fist across his eyes and slumped in his chair, deflated, defeat in his eyes. "Okay, Susie. All I can do is tell you, when you want help, we'll be here waiting. We'll do anything we can."

"We?" Susie echoed. "But Mom doesn't — " And then she guessed who he meant. "You mean your little spy-buddy, N.C.?" She saw the expression on his face and gave a brief laugh. "Sorry. Mom spilled the beans about you knowing him before. Then he admitted that you steered me onto that job because he worked there."

She wagged her head at him. "I've got a lot to thank you for, Casey." Now the bitterness sounded in her voice. She spelled it out for him. "You'll never know what a really neat place that is, the superior type people who work there. N.C.'s a good example. Is he on your payroll, maybe? Let me tell you, those folks down at Pick o' Chicken know all the angles. They're real sharp when it comes to making a little extra bread on the side."

Abruptly, Casey's face looked gray, years older. "Let me tell you something about N.C.," he began.

"Spare me." She pushed her chair back.

"Sit down, Susie!"

She had never heard him use that tone of voice before. Startled, she obeyed.

"You wouldn't let him tell you," Casey said harshly. "You're so damned wrapped up in your own troubles, it just never occurs to you that other people have things eating at them, too, things they have to live with every day for the rest of their lives."

Shock treatment, Susie thought angrily. Psyching me out now. He's tried one thing, the strong-shoulder substitute-Papa approach, and it didn't work. So now he's going to yell at me, cut me down to size.

"I'm not interested in N.C.," she said, her voice cold, "but even if I was, I wouldn't care to hear about him from you. Some friend you are. You can't wait to give me all the dirty details about something he never had a chance to tell me himself."

Casey glared at her. "He tried. But you wouldn't listen, would you? Well, you can believe this or not. The only thing N.C. ever told me was on the phone the other day. He said he tried to talk to you about why he wanted to help you, why he may be one of the few people who can understand how you feel, but you cut him off. You wouldn't listen. So he said, 'Casey, if you ever get a chance to tell her, feel free. Maybe it'll help.' "

Susie opened her mouth, then closed it. Casey had that obstinate look in his eyes. He was going to make his little speech, preach his little sermon, if he had to sit on her while he did it. She might as well let him get it off his chest and be rid of him.

In spite of herself, curiosity stirred beneath her anger.

"His name — N.C." Casey's lips twitched. "Well, I'll let him tell you that part. But he earned a nickname a few years ago to go with his initials. Never Chicken, the kids called him. Our boy has a streak of genius with cars, taking an engine apart, putting it together again, so it runs faster and smoother with more power.

He soups them up real good. At least he used to. That's how I met him, incidentally, working at a garage across town."

He sipped his cold coffee, made a face, and pushed the mug aside. "But Susie, that isn't why the nickname fit him. No, it was the way he drove a car that earned that for him. Speed happy. An addict, hopelessly hooked on fast cars, drag races, games of chicken he always won. You name it. Until the day his fast car skidded on a puddle of oil that some other car had leaked onto that empty highway, and he wrapped himself around a tree."

When he paused, Susie held her breath.

"He walked away from it with only a few scratches," Casey went on, "but his little sister didn't. Sharon's ten. She's okay now except for a scar on her forehead that'll remind them both of that particular joyride. She went through a lot of pain that N.C. won't forget in a hurry, either. Concussion, broken arm, nightmares for a long time. She still isn't eager to let N.C. drive her anywhere."

A long silence.

Susie looked down at her hands gripping each other in her lap. Don't let him get to you, she thought. He had planned this out very cleverly. Nothing else had broken through her guard, so now it was hearts and flowers time, that's all. He had come close to making the grade with this angle, though. A near miss that scared her. Because in the very next second, she knew why he was going to all this trouble, pretending he cared about her.

He wanted her out of the house.

Of course. That was it. She'd been less than enchanting to have around, no question about that. Now he was fed up. He couldn't wait another year until she went off to college. Maybe he realized, listening to her argue with Nora about medical school, that she would land in a local junior college. Then she would still be around taking up the fraction of Nora's time and attention she wasn't already spending on him.

Again she felt the ache of regret for that lost time, for the old feeling of security, of closeness to her mother.

She got to her feet. "That's a very sad story," she said, not sounding at all sad for having heard it. "But I really don't see how it would help for N.C. and me to swap confessions. Was that what you had in mind, Casey?"

His voice was quiet. "Is that all you got out of it, Susie? Is that all you heard?"

She put her head on one side as if she were thinking about it. "Well, you had quite a lot to say about people needing people," she conceded. "I think you missed a rather important point there, by the way. Because there's a — a certain responsibility involved, isn't there?

"You know, somebody told me once how much they needed me. And it was a great feeling, being needed. Until one day that person found someone else to lean on. It took a while, a long time, in fact, before I got over that, before I got it all together again."

She straightened, looking at him directly, thoughtfully. "That person was weak, that's all. Some people are like that, I suppose, going through life leaning on other people. I wouldn't want to be like that, Casey. I really wouldn't."

After a moment, he sighed. "Are you going to be strong enough to stand alone and say, 'I don't need anybody'? Do you honestly think there are many people who can manage that?"

Susie shrugged. "I haven't given it much thought."

The phone rang and she hurried to answer it, relieved to have an excuse to end the conversation that was beginning to upset her. She was delighted to hear Pam's bubbly voice on the line, the words tumbling over each other in her excitement at being home again.

"I want to hear every last little thing that's happened while I was gone."

"Let me put the dishes in to soak," Susie said. "I'll come right down. I've got so much to tell you."

She knew before she went back into the kitchen that Casey would be gone.

CHAPTER
FOURTEEN

The park party on the fourth Friday in August had been planned as a special affair, the last one before school started, a rather bittersweet celebration of the end of the summer. The girls brought food for a picnic, and the boys came with soft drinks or beer.

DeHaven and Tim offered to bring the liquor if everybody would chip in. They kept saying, looking very mysterious about it, that they had access to Greg's source of supply.

Susie thought with amusement that there sure wasn't any secret about that. Greg's father was in the wholesale liquor business. And half the kids in town knew about the store on Main Street that Greg's uncle owned.

Bob Livingston was a paunchy middle-aged type, almost bald on top, but with long, thick, graying hair to his shoulders, as well as a bushy beard. He liked to dress young, too, in way-out styles that few of the kids in Parkdale wore. But they were willing to overlook a lot about Bob Livingston. He rarely asked for an I.D., not if someone made a buy when the store was empty. Still, there was a catch to it as far as Susie was concerned. He relaxed the rules only for the boys.

Around nine o'clock that Friday night, however, she found herself thinking kindly of old Uncle Bob, chauvinist or no. She couldn't recall a better party, despite a certain awkwardness in having to avoid La Dawn and Tony. And of course she only nibbled at the food. She hadn't had any appetite since the hot weather hit.

But the music sounded marvelous, several of the guys supplying cassettes and playing them on a portable recorder. Susie danced until she wore a blister on one heel, then took off her sandals and danced barefoot. She was sure it was an evening she would never forget.

Silly. Because she must have repeated that line like a broken record. One of the new guys, somebody's cousin from Cleveland, grinned and told her, "You already said that, you know? I mean, you've said that about fourteen times. It sure is an evening we won't forget, huh, Susie?"

She leaned her head against his shoulder and laughed and laughed. He sure was a nice guy, whatever his name was. It sure was a great party. And, for sure, it was an evening she would never forget.

Through a warm golden haze she saw somebody tossing pills to Pam. Beyond, two couples were dancing on the grass.

"Oh, I want to do that! I want to dance on the grass! It would be so cool on my bare feet."

"Okay, *okay*, Susie. Cool on your bare feet. You said that already. You're pretty cool yourself, Susie. You're all right, you know that?"

Soft cool grass beneath her feet. She wondered vaguely why it didn't smell as wonderful as it used to. It had been her favorite fragrance once, newly cut grass, the greenest smell in the whole world.

She was sitting on the grass now, somebody holding her face against his bare warm chest. He moved and his medallion swung against her teeth, hurting. But that was all right. He hadn't meant to hurt her.

Someone handed her a bottle, and she drank greedily. Liquid fire, lovely liquid magic washing away all the ache inside. She choked, and the liquor ran down her chin. Overhead, faces bobbed and weaved, laughing at her. But that was all right. They were her friends, her great good friends.

She saw Pam, round face soft as she reached up to touch Scott's cheek. And somebody said, "Open your mouth and close your eyes. I'll give you a fan-TAS-tic surprise!" Popping pills in Pam's mouth.

They shouldn't do that, Susie thought dimly. But now she was caught in the dark downward spiral, legs, arms, even her voice refusing to work very well.

Something she should do, she thought. But she had forgotten what it was. What a great party. What a lovely, lovely party.

She woke to sunlight tearing at her face, shattering her eyes as if they were made of glass which fragmented from the blow of bright direct light.

A strange bedroom.

Oh, no, she thought. *Oh, no, not again —*

Then she looked up over her head and saw a shelf and something dangling over the shelf, something looking at her with one button eye.

Brotherbear!

She had only one shocked moment to realize where she was and question it, when the door opened. La Dawn came in from the hall. She stared down at Susie, her eyes huge, tragic. Was this really happening, Susie wondered, or was it the tag end of a nightmare?

She struggled to speak, but could not, her mouth as dry as if it were stuffed full of cotton.

"Susie," La Dawn said then, and her voice was infinitely gentle. "I have something to tell you."

"La Dawn!" Her voice cracked. She felt her eyes fill with tears. "Oh, I've missed you so!"

La Dawn sat down on the bed and leaned over to smooth the hair back from her forehead. "I've missed you, too, bozo. Nothing was the same, knowing I couldn't pick up the phone and — you may not be very big, but you sure left a big hole in my life."

"Same here. It's been awful."

"Monrovia Taylor cried and cried — "

"He did? Poor little kid, it wasn't his fault." Susie got up on one elbow and stayed there, even though her head was thumping horribly. "Kids say whatever they think. They just blurt it out, and when I stopped to go back over it, well, it just wasn't that big a thing. Only by then, I'd let it get all out of proportion and — "

"I know." La Dawn handed her some tissues to mop the tears. "It's okay now, Susie. That part's all okay again. But there's something else, something I have to tell you — "

Susie stared at her, trying desperately to remember last night. Something terrible must have happened. That's why La Dawn's eyes looked so stricken.

But she could only recapture blurred fragments. Dancing on the grass, laughing with somebody's cousin from Cleveland, somebody who said, "You're pretty cool, yourself, Susie."

She shook her head. "What happened? What was it? I just can't remember."

"It was Pam. Those idiots kept feeding her valium, and you know Pam, always going along with the crowd, so crazy about Scott, she'd do anything he wanted. And she was drinking vodka. In orange crush. You know how she always hated the taste of liquor. But vodka doesn't have that much taste, and they were loading her drinks."

In the echo of La Dawn's voice, the note of rage barely controlled, Susie felt a shiver of fear. *Overdose.* Pam? Little soft-faced Pam with the childlike, round gray eyes?

Why was La Dawn speaking of her in the past tense?

She couldn't ask. Her voice stuck in her throat when she tried. She could only beg with her eyes for truth, the ugly truth about last night hidden somewhere in her blacked-out memory.

La Dawn said, "Tony and I, we stayed on later than usual because — " She paused and looked at Susie uncertainly.

"Because of me? Because I passed out? Because you were worried about me, how I'd get home?" Her throat hurt, saying the words aloud, and she felt ashamed, having to say them. But that was better than making La Dawn spell it out.

It was the least she could do for her friend, sparing her that much. Because she had something to say that was much, much worse. Susie felt sure of that, even as her mind tried to add together the things that La Dawn had already said — and make the answer different.

Pam and valium and vodka —

"We just didn't feel we should leave you," La Dawn went on. "Greg Livingston was one thing, but at least he always saw that you got home. This guy from Cleveland — well, Tony said, when it came down to it, you were our responsibility. So we stayed around and then, just as we were getting you in the car, Scott came running to get me."

She straightened her slim shoulders. "He said Pam had passed out, too, but she looked funny. It scared him. The rest of them were really laughing it up because — because Pam never did that before. And those turkeys thought it was a big hilarious joke."

"Pam?" Susie said in a choked voice. "Is she all right?"

La Dawn's shoulders drooped once more. "She's bad," she said, her voice flat. "We got her to the hospital and they pumped her out, but she — Susie, she's in a coma."

She took a deep breath. "Listen. I want you to get up now. Have a cold shower or whatever will make you feel better. I mean, so you can go to the hospital with me."

Susie buried her face in the pillow. "No," she moaned, her voice muffled. "No, not Pam — "

Pictures from the past burned across her mind. Pam, running out of the house, face glowing with excitement, "Susie, Susie, you'll never guess — !"

Pam, sitting on La Dawn's bed, looking down critically at her stomach and chubby thighs. "Could I be a model, maybe? Of course I'd never be skinny enough for *clothes*."

La Dawn's hand touched her shoulder. "Come on, Susie."

"No. I'm too sick. Honestly, I can't. I just can't!"

She felt La Dawn get up from the bed. "So you're sick," she said in a tight angry voice. "Well, if you think you can hide from it, lying there with your head in the pillow, just think again. Even if I let you do it — and I won't — you'd have to face it sooner or later. For one thing, the police are questioning everybody."

Police? Susie groaned. Yes, the police would be interested in finding out what went on at that park party. They'd been watching for a long time. That's why the boys always picked somebody to act as a lookout.

"And for another thing, I think it's the least you can do as Pam's friend. Listen, after last night, I'm all through protecting you, Susie. Don't expect me to cover up for you ever again. I have had it!"

Startled, Susie peered through her fingers. Struck by a sudden thought, she asked, "What did you tell your mother? About me, I mean?"

La Dawn said shortly, "The truth."

Susie sat straight up in bed, then winced as an invisible giant rapped her on the head with concrete knuckles. "The truth?" she gasped. "What do you mean?"

"I mean, I told her you had too much to drink."

"Why on earth did you tell her that?"

La Dawn faced her, legs apart, fists on her hips, looking comically like her mother in that moment. "Because that was the truth," she said, "and it's way past time for it. I'm sick to death of lies or mousing around trying to make the truth sound different or look different — or making excuses for it. The old kidding-ourselves routine, and that's why things happen like — like what's happening to you. Like what happened to poor old Pam last night."

Susie sat, blinking, as words continued to pour out of La Dawn.

"It isn't as if she had anybody to help her a whole lot. That's what hurts. Did we help her, Susie? Did either of us help *you*? I just can't stop thinking about it."

"Yes," Susie said and thought, how could she live the rest of her life with this enormous burden along with all the rest?

"Poor Pam," La Dawn said. "Parents who couldn't have been less interested in her. *Embarrassed* about her, coming along when she did. As if there were something indecent about having a baby after a certain age. And how could anybody — not — love — Pam?"

Susie thought with an ache in her chest, she had never heard bitterness in La Dawn's voice before when she spoke about Pam's parents. Yet, she knew all too well how they felt about her. She had always known.

"There she was," La Dawn said, "a sweet little kid who hadn't grown up yet, and now she'll never get the chance. She didn't do anything so bad, did she? She wanted to be popular and make the boys like her. So she went along and did what they all did, ate what they ate and drank what they drank, putting the damned stuff in fruit wine or soda pop.

"And then some jackass came along and fed her valium. And ten minutes later, somebody gave her more, and it got to be a neat game."

La Dawn chanted, her voice rough, "Pam, the little pill-popper, dumb in the head. Now Pam's gonna be dead, dead, dead —— "

"No!" Susie clapped her hand over her mouth, aghast at the shrill agonized sound that had torn from her throat.

"You better hope yes," La Dawn said wearily.

And as Susie rocked back and forth, moaning into her cupped hands, her friend's voice went on, offering no mercy, only the stark ugly story, the aftermath of the evening no one would ever forget.

"That intern at the hospital really laid it on us. You could tell from his face that he wasn't a very hardened character yet, not about what you see on emergency room duty. He must have been hurting inside so bad that he hit out with everything he had, figuring if he made us bleed a little, too, maybe what happened to Pam wouldn't happen again.

"She might come out of that coma a vegetable, he said, her brain damaged so much she'd never be a *person* again. Or she could just stay the way she is now and waste away to fifty or sixty pounds. They look grotesque, he said, curled in the fetal position, hooked up to a bunch of machines to keep the heart pumping, the lungs working — "

"Stop it!" Susie begged. "Please stop, La Dawn. I'll go to the hospital. I promise. Only please stop telling me these things. Please — I just can't take any more."

Suddenly La Dawn's control shattered as well. With a soft strangled sob, she came blindly to the bed and held out her arms to Susie, both girls finding and sharing a measure of comfort in that embrace.

CHAPTER
FIFTEEN

A cold shower helped a little. In a borrowed
robe, Susie went back to the bedroom and got
into the shorts and blouse that La Dawn had
put out for her. Her own were wrinkled and
stained from the wet grass last night.

She had combed her hair and was smoothing
cream on her dry parched lips when someone
tapped on the door.

"Come in."

Valadia Holland fumbled with the knob and
edged her way into the room, a breakfast tray
in her hands. Her smile was easy and warm,
as always, though her dark eyes looked
troubled.

"Do you think you can eat a few bites,
Susie?"

Susie felt her eyes fill once more with burning tears. "Oh, Mrs. Holland, I don't know what to say — "

"Just say, yes, you'll try, child." Valadia's voice was soft. "And don't say any of the rest. It isn't necessary. When you stop to think about it, there isn't any one of us on this earth who's perfect." She chuckled. "Surely not in this house. I know that for a fact."

One hand gestured at the tray. "If you can't manage anything else, try to drink what's in the glass. I whipped up juice and banana and egg, and it's real soothing for the stomach. Would you just try it, honey?"

Susie gave her a trembly smile. What she really needed was a drink. But for La Dawn's mother, she would eat a six course dinner even if she died on the spot. When she sipped the frothy concoction, it did go down easily, soothing her quivering stomach just as Mrs. Holland had predicted.

Valadia nodded with approval. "Don't worry about your folks," she said. "I called them last night, told them you were staying over. I'll give your mother another call and let her know you're going to the hospital."

"Did you tell her about Pam?"

Valadia shook her head. "I'll do that this morning. Last night — well, things were pretty frantic around here. I figured it might be best to wait till we knew more about that poor baby."

She paused at the door to add, "I didn't

think it was the time to say — to say more than I did, Susie. I figure you'll know best about that, and you're the one to do it. Now, you just take your time there. La Dawn's all the help I need in the kitchen. Come down the back way. She'll be ready to leave whenever you are."

"Thank you," Susie said just above a whisper.

When the door closed again, she managed a bite or two of toast and a strip of crisp bacon. After several minutes, she got down the contents of the glass. She sat for a few more minutes to make sure her stomach would accept the small breakfast. Then she hung her bag over her shoulder and carried the tray down the back stairs to the kitchen, grateful for Mrs. Holland's tact. This way, the family gathered in the dining room wouldn't see her leave.

La Dawn was waiting for her by the back door. Quietly the two girls went down the porch steps and around the house.

A block away, Susie broke the troubled silence. "N.C. told me once I didn't know who my real friends were," she said, "and he was right. Of course he was talking about — "

"About Casey?" La Dawn smiled, catching Susie's quick glance. "Yes, I went down to talk to him one day. At the time I wasn't sure it was the right thing to do, but somebody straightened me out about that."

Susie felt a flick of anger, but it died away as

quickly as it had flared within her. She must still be in shock, she thought. Nothing seemed to matter too much anymore, none of the negative things, anyway. Well, that was all right. Maybe it was time to concentrate on the positive things left in her life. La Dawn was one of them.

"Was it your mom?" she asked. "Did you talk to her about me — before you talked to Casey?"

La Dawn nodded. "I didn't mention any names, but I'm sure she knew who I meant. She's pretty sharp that way."

"She didn't seem to be upset with me," Susie said slowly. "No, that isn't the right word. She cares. Your mom always seems to care about people. But it was as if she — accepted everything. Pam, me, all of it. She wasn't disgusted or shocked or horrified, and she didn't make judgments all over the place like — like most people would."

La Dawn gave a short laugh. "Pretty shockproof, my mom. But you're right, she does accept things. And people. I suppose families like mine learn to face things somewhere along the line, to face facts. You try to do something about a situation if you can. And if you can't, you try not to let it bother you too much."

They stopped for a light at Main Street, crossed it, and walked on through another residential section, this one older than their own, not as well cared for. Many of the big three-story houses had a weathered look, paint peeling from the siding, signs in the window offering rooms to rent.

The sun was already too hot for comfort, though a faint breeze stirred occasionally, lifting Susie's bangs from her damp forehead. Her stomach hurt now, a steady grinding pain as if she'd swallowed little pieces of glass along with those few bites of food.

"You okay?" La Dawn asked, leaning over to look at her closely.

Susie nodded. "I'm dreading it, that's all. Seeing Pam."

It was almost a relief when the girl at the hospital admitting desk shook her head firmly, denying their request.

"No visitors," she said in a voice that sounded indifferent to anything except the rules of the place. "No one but family."

Susie looked at La Dawn as they turned away. Then she saw her face change as she sucked in her breath.

"Look. There they are. That's her sister with them."

Pam's mother and father came down the hall, their faces identical still in this bleak, dazed moment of comprehension.

Mrs. Lyon saw them first, paused, then came toward them with small hurried steps. "You girls," she said and reached out to them with a white-gloved hand clutching a sodden handkerchief. "Tell me how it happened," she pleaded. "How could a thing like this happen to our little girl?"

La Dawn made a slight helpless movement. Susie could only stand in stunned silence.

"Pam wasn't ever on drugs," Mrs. Lyon said, her head moving slowly from side to side. "Never! She thought drugs were terrible. You know that — you, Susie and — La Dawn. You were her friends! You've been friends so long, for all these years — "

"Mother, please," her older daughter murmured.

Mr. Lyon took his wife's arm in an ineffectual attempt at calming her. She shook off his hand, pursuing her point with some desperate singleminded need.

Susie thought dully, how could she offer comfort when she couldn't be sure what Mrs. Lyon wanted to hear? What could she say?

Within a frozen sense of her own inadequacy, her consuming guilt, she heard her voice, full of tears. "I'm so sorry. I'm so awfully sorry — "

Mrs. Lyon drew herself up, and her red-rimmed eyes narrowed behind the gold-framed glasses. "Yes," she said, "you were such good friends. So why didn't you help her when she needed help? Where were you when this terrible thing happened?"

"*Please,* Mother," her daughter said in a firm controlled voice. This time she managed to step in front of the woman and turn her

148

aside. With her father's help, she led her mother away. But their eyes flickered over the girls' faces as they passed, and the expression in them clearly echoed those bitter accusing words.

Yes, why didn't you help her?

Susie closed her eyes and let out her breath in a soundless sigh. Then she jumped as she heard her name.

The head nurse, Julia Shaw, stood a few feet away. But her mother's friend was not smiling today as she had been when she brought the beautiful Pendleton pantsuit to the house. Stern, tight-lipped, she studied the girls before she spoke again.

"Would you like to see your friend for a moment?"

"Oh, yes. Yes, we would," Susie blurted. "Could we?"

The white-capped head dipped in a brief nod. "I think it might be a very good idea. Come along."

La Dawn looked at Susie, eyebrows raised. Then, silently, they walked down the corridor behind the figure in the crisp uniform. Mrs. Shaw stopped at last in front of a door bearing a 'No Visitors' sign. She pushed it open and stepped inside so the girls could follow her into the room.

There was only one bed, so there was really no place to look but at the girl who lay upon it. Still, Susie mentally noted the things in that stark antiseptic place with a compulsive sense of duty about it, as if she were here to observe so that someone could test her later.

Bed, metal table with a drawer and cabinet beneath. On the table, a long syringe with a bulb at one end. Beside the table, a chair covered with green fabric. A wheeled lunch tray. And by the bed, the I.V. apparatus like some modern sculptor's idea of a long-legged bird, bottle in beak. From that bottle fluid dripped into the rounded arm of the girl lying there, so still, so pale, a tube in her nose. The hospital gown stirred slightly with each breath. It was the only indication that she was alive.

Susie blinked through the tears streaming down her face. She put out her hand, but it stopped in midair as if it had decided all on its own that her touch might be contaminating. At last, with the tips of her fingers, she touched one lock of the blonde hair fanned out across the pillow.

Memory stirred. Again she saw Pam before the mirror in her bedroom, brushing that long hair, then standing back to say with real despair, "My hair is absolutely the only thing I have going for me. It would be so neat to be pretty!"

They had teased her, of course, because it was fun to tease Pam. She reacted beautifully, volatile and tragic about the flaws she loved to dramatize.

Susie had said, "Oh, Pammy, you're gorgeous *inside*. You just can't have it both ways unless you invent reversible skin or something."

And La Dawn drawled, "If they ever take X-rays of your liver they'll get published in *Playboy,* hear?"

Oh, why hadn't they told her she was pretty?

"I think you'd better leave now," Mrs. Shaw said, and her face relaxed the least bit.

Susie swallowed against the hard bitter lump in her throat. "Will she — ?"

The nurse shook her head. "I don't know," she said. She put her hand on Susie's arm. "I went against the rules, letting you see her. But I want you to go back — and tell those kids who were at the party. Tell them what you saw."

Susie nodded and murmured her thanks for La Dawn, too, because she saw that La Dawn couldn't speak. By mutual consent they walked down the hall in the other direction so they could go out the side door. Outside they headed for a nearby bench, sat down and cried painfully, wrenchingly, on each other's shoulders.

Susie ached with the need for a drink. And mixed in with that insistent gnawing hunger was guilt. At a time like this, all she could think about was getting home to that bottle.

"Maybe Pam's lucky," she said and blew her nose. "With a friend like me, she sure didn't need any enemies. Why didn't I help her? Well, that's the laugh for today. I can't even help myself."

"You want help?" La Dawn took a deep

tremulous breath. "I've been waiting a long time to hear you say that."

Susie put her head down on the low back of the bench. "I think I want to die. That's what I really want."

"Only sixteen years on you, and you're ready to cash it in already?" But La Dawn's voice sounded a little unsteady, and panic flashed briefly in her dark eyes.

"I'm really a rotten person. You know that."

La Dawn relaxed against the bench and laughed, the funny gurgling laugh that showed she was genuinely amused. "Most people have a few bad spots here and there," she commented, "but a few flaky types like you, bozo, get the idea you're winning all the medals for pure inspired badness. Listen, you've only been working at it a few months. You're nowhere near being even slightly sinful."

"You don't know everything I've done."

"And what's more, I don't want to hear about it," La Dawn said briskly. "No way am I going to be your mother confessor. I just want you to think about one thing. If I don't know what you've been doing out there, wallowing in badness, well, you don't know about anyone else, either. You've got no way of knowing the stuff other people tote around on their backs. Just because they don't do a lot of talking about it doesn't mean it isn't marked in big letters down deep inside them. On their souls, I guess."

She added resignedly, "I suppose you got a white soul, too. Well, I won't hold that against you, just because I happen to think black is better."

Susie lifted her head and smiled faintly. Trust La Dawn to make her feel better, even about herself. Funny, though. She was saying practically the same thing that Casey said the other day, the day he told her about N.C. Casey, of all people.

Through a great dragging weariness she said, "I'm so mixed up. I wonder if I'll ever get my head straight." She stared at La Dawn. "You've had it together for a long time. Tell me, how will I know — if I ever get there?"

La Dawn's laugh sounded vaguely embarrassed. "Bozo, you come out with the heaviest questions. What can I tell you? Well, okay, there's this that my mom told me once. And Valadia is one very wise lady. She says there's a long period in growth when a person expects more from other people than he does from himself. Little kids, right? And kids our age. Maturity, that's the point when you reverse it — when you expect more from yourself than anybody else."

"Mmm," Susie said, nodding. "Yeah, that's good. Good, but not easy."

La Dawn chuckled. "Some people never get there," she pointed out, her voice amused. "But I like to think it's because they never really try.

153

It's a lot easier when you blow it to blame other people."

Her fingers curled around Susie's hand. "Can you think about one more thing? You love Pam, you love me. When are you going to start loving Susie? First of all, you've got to forgive yourself for all this sinning around. I mean, who's perfect? Not you or me, not even Casey." She mumbled something Susie didn't catch.

"He talked to me," Susie said. Her voice drifted off as she thought about the things Casey had said. She thought about Nora then and winced, picturing a scene in which she told her mother the truth. Her mind recoiled from that, and the pain must have shown in her face.

La Dawn squeezed her hand again. "One step at time," she said softly. "Nobody has to be alone unless they want it that way. When you need help, Susie — reach out for it."

Susie took a deep shaky breath. "I'd better get home." She stood up. "I don't know about the rest," she said vaguely. "I'll try. I promise you that, La Dawn. I'll try."

Yet, even as they started home, she was thinking, sick with self-contempt, if she could have just one drink from the bottle in her bathroom cupboard, then maybe she could figure out what to do.

CHAPTER
SIXTEEN

She let herself in the front door as quietly as she could, but her mother called to her from the kitchen. She must have been listening for the squeaky board on the porch, Susie thought, and resigned herself to the inevitable delay in getting upstairs.

"Susie? Come out to the kitchen, honey." She smiled when Susie appeared in the doorway, but it was not a very permanent looking smile. And her eyes were bright with tears.

"Honey, I'm so sorry about Pam, so awfully sorry — "

Strange, Susie thought. That was practically the same thing she had said to Pam's mother. Is that what people said about death or something almost as terrible? When they couldn't come up with anything better, more helpful or

155

comforting, is that what they said?

I'm so sorry, so awfully sorry —

She must have made some reply, because Nora nodded.

"Her poor mother," she said, then shook herself and gestured toward the table.

Casey sat there, turned slightly as if he had glanced around when she came into the kitchen. But now he sat staring into the steaming contents of his coffee mug, lips pursed, eyes thoughtful.

"Sit down, darling," Nora said. "I'm just getting lunch on the table."

Susie felt her stomach quiver. "Lunch?" she said. "Oh, nothing for me, thanks. I had a late breakfast at La Dawn's."

"Well, this is a late lunch," her mother said firmly. "I want to talk to you, dear. Sit down and drink a cup of soup, anyway."

Head on one side, she studied her daughter. "These crazy diets of yours! How often have I told you that they can be dangerous! You're really much too thin now."

Reluctantly, Susie sat down. She looked at Casey, still brooding over his coffee, but he didn't look at her. In the next moment she found herself studying him, at first because she didn't want to see the traces of tears on her mother's face. And then she found her interest caught and held by the strands of gray in Casey's black curly hair.

How long had they been there? She hadn't

noticed before, nor had she seen the lines etched in his broad forehead, the deep grooves between his nostrils and the corners of his mouth.

They would disappear when he smiled, those lines carved in flesh. But Casey didn't smile much any more. She thought, bemused, right now he looked like a man with big worries on his mind. She wondered vaguely what he was so worried about.

As if he felt her silent inspection, he looked up and gave her a faint ghost of his former go-to-hell grin.

"Good morning."

Susie nodded. "Back at you," she said and realized, startled, that there was a subtle difference in the sound and feel of the exchange. Why was that? Wasn't it the way they usually greeted each other, in ordinary words and phrases, in an easy neutral tone?

But Casey was already staring in his cup once more, lost in deep inner reflection. So the difference, whatever it was, must be in her. Abruptly, Susie knew what it was. This morning she wasn't looking at him with her usual hostility.

It was as if her inner turmoil during the past few hours had flattened all her old emotions. There simply wasn't room inside for anything else. Drained of tears, she lacked energy to pump up those former strong feelings, certainly not about Casey. Not right this minute, anyway. She had other problems that were far more pressing. And she was terribly tired.

Nora put a cup of soup in front of her where the tomato and spice aroma made its way instantly to Susie's nose. She felt a dizzying wave of nausea and leaned back, breathing carefully through her mouth.

"Much too thin," her mother repeated in the same clucking tone. "Diets! At your age!"

Susie felt a prickle of irritation. She shoved the soup a few inches away. For a moment Mrs. Lyon's voice echoed in her ears.

"Our little girl," it said. *"How could a thing like this happen to our little girl?"*

Overnight that little girl had become a big girl with all the problems that went with age and stature, king-sized problems and giant problems and jumbo economy-sized problems. So when would it be Big Girl Time on South Elm Street in Parkdale? In the wake of that absurd question flickering across her mind came a flash of real anger.

She looked up at her mother and saw that she was smiling indulgently, and that her eyes were quite dry now. "Where did you ever get the idea that I've been on a diet?" she asked.

Her voice was quiet, but the taut sound of it erased Nora's smile. She looked faintly puzzled.

Casey's head jerked up, blue eyes alert.

Nora gave a short laugh. "Well, you've certainly been giving every indication. Eating like a bird, I mean." She frowned. "Of course in this ghastly heat, nobody's appetite is up to par. Susie, are you feeling all right?"

The anger inside grew, mixed in with the pain that usually made her sick and blind to everything except that silent need. Forget it, she told herself. What kind of crummy world was it where something so awful could happen to Pam?

And here *she* sat at the old kitchen table, a table with marks on the far end where she'd kicked it when she was in her highchair. She was okay, sitting here. Nothing had happened to her, even though she'd been busy all summer pigging down all the booze she could get her hands on. She was all right, even after all the things she'd done to get it.

"What did you say, dear?"

"I said, it should have been me," Susie repeated loudly. "I should be the one lying there with a tube in my nose and that junk dripping in my vein."

"Oh, honey, I know how you feel. I know how it must have upset you." Nora paused. Faint lines appeared on her forehead. "You mean — you mean they let you in to see her? Well, I certainly question the wisdom of that." She sounded indignant. "Who was on the floor, anyway?"

Susie leaned back and stared at her, wondering what it would take to make Nora really see her, not just a montage of all the cunning little

Susies from babyhood to somewhere around age ten. Obviously at about that point, Nora's concept of her daughter had stopped growing and changing.

The flame of anger grew, its heat rising through her chest to touch her throat. Her voice sounded raw and husky. "Mrs. Shaw let us in. She said it was against the rules. But she wanted us to go back and tell all the kids, everybody at that party, just what we saw."

Nora looked away abruptly from whatever it was she glimpsed in Susie's face. She glanced at Casey and paused for a few seconds, lips parted, as she saw his expression. He was watching Susie closely now, the mug of coffee still in his hand.

"Well!" Nora commented coolly. "She takes a lot on herself, I must say. And what good did it do? Did it help find the person who slipped those pills to Pam? Anybody who would do something so stupid, so criminal — but of course, it'll never come out, who it was."

"Who they were, you mean," Susie said. She had a strange sensation that something outside herself had taken over, something she couldn't control. But it didn't matter. She rode with the cresting wave of anger.

"There were several people at that party giving pills to Pam," she said, "and loading her drinks. In orange crush or that yucky fruit wine. You can't taste liquor too much that way. And Pam never liked the taste of liquor."

160

There was horror on her mother's face, fear in her eyes. "You — you *saw* all that going on? But why — why didn't you — ?"

"Why didn't I do anything about it? Good question. Why didn't I help her? Actually, that's just what Pam's mother wanted to know. We bumped into her in the hospital and that's just what she asked us. 'You were her friends,' she said. 'Why didn't you help her?'"

She felt a warm wet drop on her hands folded in her lap and looked down, surprised. She hadn't realized she was crying again. She had thought all her tears were used up by now.

"Mother," she said and took a ragged breath. "I'll tell you the truth. La Dawn says it's time we started telling the truth, and she's absolutely right. The reason I didn't help Pam is quite simple. I was drunk."

The words seemed to hang in the hot still air. After a few seconds, she heard Casey sigh softly.

Nora stood motionless, no movement on her face except for the tears slowly gathering in her eyes. "Oh, my poor baby," she whispered at last. "How awful for you! But, Susie, don't you see, you mustn't feel such terrible guilt. It wasn't your *fault*!"

"Tell me, Mother, whose fault was it?"

"Well, those people, whoever they were, who put the pills in Pam's — in whatever she was drinking."

"That isn't the way it happened, Mother.

They just gave her the pills, and she swallowed them quite happily." She pushed back the picture that evoked and went on in the same even tone. "So if it isn't my fault because I just sat there and let it happen — and those people who gave the pills to Pam aren't to blame, either, because nobody forced her to take them — well, don't you see? That means, when it comes right down to it, Pam's the only one left. Was it her fault, Mother?"

"She'd been drinking," Nora said harshly, then made an unbelieving gesture, hands to her face, as if the meaning of her words had hit her abruptly, brutally.

Susie made a soft sound. "And so had I," she said. "And so had I. Until I passed out and woke up in La Dawn's bed. So it was a very sad thing for Pam if she depended on old buddy Susie for any help."

"Oh, stop it!" Nora said crossly. "You act like you're really enjoying this — this recital of sins. Hurting me, throwing it in my face. Well, I won't let you do it. You went to a party, and you got drunk. Okay, I hope you've learned a lesson.

"Sure, it's sad and terrible that the party had a tragic ending. But let me straighten you out, young lady. The whole burden isn't on your shoulders just because you did a very silly thing last night. It won't help one bit to dramatize the fact that you were foolish enough to have too much to drink. Unfortunately that's a part of growing pains. You aren't the first, and you won't be the last. Everybody has to try it at least once."

Susie laughed, a shrill unpleasant sound. "You just won't listen to what I'm saying," she said. "I'm not trying to make it easier for myself, either. And, believe me, I don't want to hurt you any more than — Mother, listen to me! Last night wasn't the first time — or the tenth — or the fortieth. I've been drinking all summer, since before school let out, in fact. *Oh, please don't look at me like that!* I'm trying to tell you — I can't stop — I can't help it — *I can't stop!*"

She reached blindly for her mother, but the hand that grasped hers was Casey's. When she blinked away the tears, she saw Nora backing away, her face white, contorted.

"Oh, no!" she said hoarsely. "What would your father say? If he could see you now, what would — ?"

"Damn it, Nora, that's enough!" Casey roared, on his feet now, still gripping Susie's hand. "I've tried to keep out of this, but now you've gone too far. How can you tear her apart at the very moment she's finally brought herself to ask for help?"

His wife turned on him to say bitterly, "Sure. Go on, throw it at me. Say 'I told you so.' Be righteous!"

Casey's head went back as if she had struck him.

Susie thought she felt a slight tremor in his fingers, an echo of the pain she saw on his face. Why — he did care about her! She had laughed at him, even sneered at him, subtly, gone out of her way to give him a hard time. Yet, here he was, sticking up for her, trying to help.

No, not Casey! She must be imagining things. After the way she acted, why would he lift a finger to help her?

"She's your daughter," he said to Nora, a plea in his voice.

"My baby — " she faltered.

"No! Not your baby. Take another look. She's almost a woman. But she's your daughter, and something more, a lot more than an extension of you and her father."

He held out his other hand. "She's a person in her own right, Nora," he said. "And she needs you now more than she's ever needed you in all her sixteen years."

Susie couldn't take her eyes off his face as he stood watching her mother. Because his voice had broken on the last words, and she saw the glimmer of tears in his eyes.

Sobbing, Nora came at last to put her arms around Susie. And it seemed right that Casey shared that embrace. She had been wrong about a lot of things, Susie thought, and felt something akin to awe, realizing how mistaken she had been about Casey.

Nora drew away at last with a little strangled

laugh and went to the pantry to get a box of tissues.

Her knees suddenly buckling, Susie sat down. She gave Casey a watery smile. Then she said quickly, almost stammering, "Please — please go get it now before I change my mind. I'm not — strong enough to do it myself."

Just like always, he read her mind. "Where is it, Susie?"

"Up in my bathroom cupboard. Below the sink. In the bottle that says — rubbing alcohol."

He nodded, touched her cheek. "Thanks."

As he went out of the kitchen, she sagged against the back of the chair. He had understood that, too, she thought, and accepted it, the gift she had just given him.

CHAPTER
SEVENTEEN

Brookhaven.

As she lay across her bed late that afternoon, Susie reflected on the name of the place where she would go in the morning, where she would be staying for the next few weeks. Brookhaven sounded like a place in the country, a huge rambling house with trees and lots of lawn around it and, naturally, a brook nearby.

But Casey had described it to her, and she knew now that what he had once told her was true. He would never lie to her.

So she listened closely when he said, "It's in Chicago, Susie, on the West Side, a big old house sort of like this one, but on a larger lot. And it's something in between a hospital and a nursing home, a place for alcoholics, women alcoholics."

She wondered at the time if he knew what a jolt that word gave her, if that were the reason he said it over and over, as a way to get her used to it.

That's what she was, of course. An alcoholic. He had told her that, he and Nora, looking sorry about it but not disgusted or horrified any more than La Dawn's mother had been. Nora had turned very pale, her eyes a bit dazed, but once she recovered from the first shock, she rallied to sit over endless cups of coffee (hot milk and a mild sedative for Susie). They discussed what had happened to her over the last few months. And Nora, biting her lip occasionally, was honest about what she could expect at Brookhaven.

Nobody knew for sure why some people were alcoholics, they said. Maybe it was an inherited weakness like a susceptibility to certain diseases, passed from one generation to another in the genetic chain. It could also be an accident of nature creating a chemical imbalance in certain people.

Whatever the cause, it was nothing to be ashamed of, Casey said firmly. There were great statesmen and scientists and writers and actors who were alcoholics, who lived long productive lives, happy and healthy on the AA program.

The AA people had been contacted too, and a girl had come right out to talk to her. Becky was a pretty blonde who looked from here about Susie's age, though she turned out to be nineteen. She had been dry for two years now, she said, and that meant there had been two birthday cakes for her at the AA meetings, one for each year.

"You'll like the people, Susie," she said. "It's a young group, a couple of the kids younger than you. Oldest guy there is twenty-three. We had the crazy idea, just like you did, that alcoholics are all middle-aged types."

"Yeah," Susie said. "Boy, was that a mistake." She felt a lot better, though, knowing she'd be with kids close to her age. She wasn't kidding herself about what lay ahead. She didn't feel very good right now, and it would get worse during the days to come.

One thing might make it easier, Susie thought. When she came back, it would be like a new beginning here at home with Casey and Nora. At school, senior year would be really neat. And there was N.C. —

Susie rolled over on the bed, closed her eyes, and drifted again, remembering the phone call. Casey must have let him know what happened, but that was all right. Hearing N.C.'s voice, cheerful and funny and happy for her, gave her a tremendous lift. She hadn't realized how much she had missed him.

"Hey kid, I hear you're going out of town for a while. I wanted to check if it's okay if I — if I write to you."

"Oh, N.C., that would be great."

"Yeah, well, there's a lot to tell you. I'm in a new job. I mean, actually, I'm back at the old one. At the garage. I got my head straight about a few things, and this is better bread. So I can take you out on the town when you get back. To celebrate." He laughed. "Steak and salad and soda pop. Okay?"

"Sounds fantastic."

"We're going to have a lot to talk about," he said, sounding serious.

"Yes."

"There's only one thing — "

"What?"

"Well, I want everything up front between us from now on. Okay?"

"Sure."

"Then I think you'd better know something."

She waited, frowning, anxious now.

His voice came at last, sounding subdued, far away. "My name," he said. "N.C. stands for — Norville Chalmers — "

"Oh," she said after a moment. "*Oh, N.C.* — "

Someone tapped at the door very softly. It opened a few inches, then wider as La Dawn poked her head around it.

"Hey, bozo, you're supposed to be sleeping."

Susie lifted a hand in greeting. "I've been asleep. I'm just lying here thinking. Come on in. You're just the cure for a sprained brain."

La Dawn flopped on the other bed and handed Susie a shoebox tied up with red ribbon. "Brought you a going-away present."

"You heard about Brookhaven?"

La Dawn nodded. "Sounds beautiful." She grinned. "You look all laid back, just thinking about it. Well, that's to remind you of us." She waved at the shoebox. "He'll keep you company so you won't get homesick."

Before she untied the ribbon, Susie guessed what she would find. Brotherbear lay inside on a bed of white tissue paper, peering amiably up at her with his one button eye.

"Oh, La Dawn, thank you! I'll take such good care of him!"

"Sure you will. But he's all yours now for as long as you need him. I finally figured him out, you know? What he is, he's a groovin' little symbol. He stands for what happens when people try to change other people."

She pointed with one slim finger. "What is he, anyway? He sure isn't a brown and black panda like I wanted him to be. He's a panda with brown shoe polish on him. Always has been. I finally realized nobody can change anybody else, not really. You can only change yourself."

Susie sighed. "Yeah," she agreed. "Well, I hope he'll help. I'm gonna have one tremendous remodeling job."

"One thing at a time," La Dawn said comfortably, lying back to prop one bare brown foot on top of the other knee. "Now that you've got a few things straight, such as how good a dude Casey really is, well, you can houseclean your head any time you get around to it."

"Mmm," Susie said. "Maybe it's the tranquilizer, but I don't think I'm mad about anything any more. Or so awfully scared. La Dawn, you know something? I've been mad about a lot of things for a long, long time."

"That was the start of it," La Dawn said. "My mom says that can eat at you real good."

Susie stared at the ceiling. "What a waste. A whole summer. It's like a blur when I try to remember. I've gone and lost a whole summer out of my life."

"So what's a summer?" La Dawn said. "You win some, you lose some. I think maybe you're on the way to finding yourself. That's what's important."

If she got lost again, Susie thought, it was great to know one thing. She wouldn't have to fight her way back alone. La Dawn was right about that. All she had to do was reach out for help.